CRUISIN
FOR A
BRUISIN

CRUISIN
FOR A
BRUISIN

Winifred Rosen

ALFRED A. KNOPF ⟩⟩⟩ NEW YORK

To Jacob Brackman
with gratitude and love

THIS IS A BORZOI BOOK PUBLISHED BY ALFRED A. KNOPF, INC.

Library of Congress Cataloging in Publication Data
Casey, Winifred Rosen, 1943– Cruisin for a Bruisin
  SUMMARY: The thirteen-year-old daughter of a psychoanalyst describes her growing sexual awareness and her intense relationships with boys and her family.
  I. Title. PZ7.C26815Iah3 [Fic] 76–5488 ISBN 0–394–83291–4

CRUISIN
FOR A
BRUISIN

FIRST

LATELY I'VE BEGUN TO think that everyone is crazy. I'm not sure when it started, but since I turned thirteen—six months ago —I've been more and more sure that I understand less and less well what is really going on.

Take sex, for example—not that I *ever* understood it, no matter how many people tried explaining it to me—but I never used to *worry* about it.

My mother worried about it—constantly, she says. As soon as we were old enough to talk, she started worrying about how she was going to explain sex to her children. A couple of years went by before I asked her, as she was putting on my mittens, where babies came from. She went running to my father, who sent her back to tell me. My mother must have

1

been too uncomfortable with the subject to do it justice. I can't remember her explanation. What I said was: "Where's my other mitten?"

A few years later, our second grade teacher, Irene, brought the whole class into the Nature Room. Janet, I remember, played with the tiny, red-eyed mice, and Roger teased me with a snake.

In the corner was the rabbit cage with five teensie, pink rabbit babies that no one was allowed to touch.

Irene had silvery-streaked hair and milky skin. She said, "Attention everyone, you too, Winnie. I want everyone to sit around the table."

Everyone sat around the table.

"Today," she announced, "we're going to talk about the way babies are made."

We all glanced at each other and bit our lips.

Irene produced a chart, which she unrolled and hung in front of the blackboard. It was in color, showing the reproductive organs of a female person. With her pencil, Irene located two small whitish objects and informed us that they were called ovaries. The ovaries, she said, produced an ovum every month. She asked me what I thought an ovum was.

The blood, I remember, was pounding in my ears. I did not like the drift of the conversation. A conversation like that could easily lead to the mention of certain words it would be better to leave unmentioned.

I said, no, I didn't know. She said, "Think of an oval, an ovum is something with an oval shape."

Roger hooked his thumbs under his armpits and flapped his elbows up and down.

"Oh," I said, "an egg."

The egg, she told us, traveled through a little tube into the uterus. She spelled uterus.

"The uterus," she said, "is where babies are made."

She unrolled another chart. This one of a man.

I looked at the table and repeated, "U-T-E-R-U-S," to myself, over and over to keep from laughing.

"Men are made differently from women," Irene informed us. "They do not have ovaries or little tubes or uteruses. What is more, men have their reproductive organs on the *outside* of their bodies."

Now, long before, when I was a very small child, my grandmother read me a story about a little boy who had a special kind of rubber ball that had been invented by a mad scientist. Once the ball was bounced, it would keep on bouncing, higher and higher, until nobody could stop it and it would go crashing through the ceiling. The mad scientist warned the little boy never to bounce the ball, but of course the little boy had to *prove* that it really would bounce higher and higher and crash through the ceiling, and it did.

Listening to Irene explain how millions of little sperm are produced in a man's testes made me feel just like that ball. I dug my nails into my palms, bit the insides of my cheeks, and prayed for self-control.

"Now," said Irene, clearing her throat, "the sperm have to get from the father's testes into the mother's uterus where the egg is waiting to be

3

fertilized. Otherwise no babies can be made."

I wished no babies would be made. Not here, at least. Not while *I* was in the room.

Irene cleared her throat again. Janet was staring at the table and everybody, even Roger, was as quiet as red-eyed mice.

"During intercourse," Irene finally announced, "the man puts his—"

My laughter exploded like a bomb and the next word never got spoken.

"Winifred!" said Irene, "*control* yourself."

I tried.

I failed.

She grew desperate. "All right now," she commanded, "this will have to stop. Turn your chair around this minute."

This only made me giggle harder.

I tried holding my breath.

"That's better," said Irene. "Now, as I was saying, the man, during intercourse, puts his—Winifred! Tell me: *What is so funny?*"

Her question struck me as the stupidest I had ever heard, and I fell, crashing off my chair onto the floor, gasping for breath, into a trembling heap under the table.

The reason they sent me home from school was that I had hiccups, which nobody could stop, not even Dr. Julia.

My mother wanted to know what happened.

"Nothing. I was—*hic*—laughing, that's all," I

told her, my stomach in a knot of apprehension.

"What were you laughing at?"

"*Hic!*"

"Don't you want to talk about it?"

"Yes. No. *Hic!*"

Later on my father came home. "What's the matter?" he asked me.

"I have hiccups," I said.

"Did you try drinking backwards out of a glass?"

"Yes."

"Turn a somersault?"

"*Hic!* Uh-huh."

"BOO!" he said.

"They tried that too," I told him.

"Tell me," he said seriously, "what was happening when you started hiccuping?"

"I don't want to," I said.

"Did something embarrass you?"

"No!"

"Something someone talked about in school?"

"Go away!"

"Let's see, it must have been something important. . . ."

"Daddy!" I yelled, "I don't want to talk about it and *I'm not kidding!*"

It was impossible to go to sleep with hiccups. I went to talk to my parents.

"What's the matter? Can't you go to sleep?" my mother asked.

"The hiccups make it hard."

"Poor bunny," she said.

"The bunny had babies, Mommy, did I tell you?"

"No. How many babies did the bunny have?"

"Five. But we're not allowed to touch them. They're tiny."

"All babies are tiny," my mother said.

"Not hippopotamuses' babies," I told her. "They weigh as much as I do now."

"Did you learn that in school, dear?" my mother inquired.

"No. I never learn anything in school."

"Is that true?" my father asked. "Never? Anything?"

"Only a little. Sometimes."

"Like what?"

"U-T-E-R-U-S. That's the way you spell uterus."

My parents exchanged glances.

"Any other interesting little tidbits of information?" my father wanted to know.

"I don't remember any."

"Let me understand this," he said. "One day somebody came into your classroom, told you how to spell uterus, and left?"

"Not exactly. Irene told us how babies are made."

"That would explain the part about the uterus, then."

"I didn't mind that part."

"Which part did you mind?"

"The way . . . the-way-the-sperms-get-from-the-father-into-the-mother," I said as fast as I could, feeling a wave of relief when it was out.

"You mean," my father said, "the part that goes, 'The man puts his—'"

6

"YES!" I told him, "that's it!"

"Of course," he smiled, "after all, that's the funny part."

"I know it!" I almost shouted, "but that's what I don't understand!"

"What?"

"How people *do* it without laughing."

"They don't think about it," he said. "It's only funny if you think about it. If you *do* it, it's different."

I'm still not sure I could do it with a straight face. Not that I've ever done it. 'Cause I haven't.

1

Castro was reported alive and fighting in the Cuban hills, so it isn't true, as everyone was saying, that he's dead.

This afternoon ten thousand kids are rioting in Times Square after waiting for eighteen and a half hours to see a creepy disk jockey named Alan Freed do a show on Rock 'n' Roll.

But something even more monumental happened on this last Saturday in February, 1957, which is that my older sister Diana got her hair cut.

Right now, she is standing in front of her mirror in a trance. "Well," she finally says, "what do you think?"

There is no question of telling the truth. "It looks terrific," I say.

I feel a fleeting sense of grief for the lost beauty of her hair—very fleeting—followed by a surge of satisfaction: my enemy's chief weapon has been destroyed, hacked off by the shears of some secret ally. The few inches that remain have been permanented into frizzy curls. "How come you decided to do it?" I wonder.

"What do you mean, 'how come'? Don't you like it?" she snaps insecurely.

"I told you, I like it."

"Everyone's getting their hair cut. I think short hair's cute and more sophisticated, don't you?"

"Much." I feel guilty. It is not nice of me to want my sister to look ugly just because she is so pretty. And yet, it is what I have always hoped would happen. Because I have felt funny-looking ever since I can remember, I guess; ever since I was a pudgy baby who made everybody laugh. Lately, it is worse than ever because I have unruly mouse-brown hair, braces straightening out my bottom teeth, and (worst of all) practically no shape at all.

Diana is reaching for a tube of lipstick and smearing it onto her lips. It is oily orange, her favorite. After rubbing her lips together, she pulls at the curls on top of her head and frowns. Wow, I think, she looks awful!

She is wearing a blue boatneck sweater over a white button-down shirt. The pleats of a gray wool skirt cover most of her knees, nearly meeting the tops of her white socks. She has dimes in her loafers.

9

"Winnie," she says, turning toward me with a worried expression. "Are you *sure*? How long do you think it'll take to grow out?"

"What do you want it to do that for?" (I panic at the thought of her being beautiful again in just a few short months.)

"Because I look hideous this way!"

"Diana, you're being crazy."

"Do you know what you are?" she says, hands on her hips, her eyes narrowing angrily. "A little fink! Get out of my room." The clench of her jaw is menacing.

"What did *I* do?"

"I know what you really think, you little creep. You're *happy* I'm ugly!"

"You're crazy," I say.

She takes a step forward, her hands forming fists. "If you don't get out of here in exactly three seconds . . ."

Three seconds later I am gone, banished to an extra maid's room, which is my room in our new apartment. Diana has a large front room, overlooking Central Park and facing into the glorious morning sun. This is fair because when I was a baby I had everything my way, and Diana had to sleep in my father's study. Now that I am thirteen Diana isn't making any more sacrifices for me. Besides, I annoy her. For example: chewing my toast in the morning. The way I breathe also annoys her.

In my room I decide to play my guitar. I am not so good at guitar-playing, and whenever I try to get better, Diana gets annoyed.

The door crashes open.

"Be quiet!" she commands. "I'm studying!"

I pretend to be engrossed in my chord chart.

"And don't *bug* me!" Slam.

I play on.

This time she enters raving irrationally: "If you don't stop that vile noise, I'm getting Father!"

"Get him," I say. "He's in his office."

His office is part of our apartment because my father is a psychoanalyst.

"Soon he'll be out of his office!" she threatens.

"Good for him," I say. "All I'm doing is practicing. I have to practice, don't I?"

"Not like that, and not while I'm studying."

"You're not studying. You're looking at your cute, sophisticated hair."

"You are a hypocritical little pig and don't ever bother asking me for anything ever again."

"Okay."

"And that goes for my green skirt, too."

"But that's not *fair*! You already wore my—"

"That," she interrupts, "is just too bad," and closes the door soundlessly.

My father once told me that the reason people become psychoanalysts is that they are crazy and want to know why. My father doesn't seem crazy to me, though. Maybe his craziness was psychoanalyzed out of him long ago. My mother was never psychoanalyzed, and my father says she is still as crazy as ever.

My mother grew up in a big family on Long Island, and whenever anybody got annoyed or angry or depressed they were advised to go out and get some fresh air. Going out for some fresh air is still my mother's top remedy, even though my father spent twelve years studying to be a psychoanalyst. She is long-limbed and daringly attractive, I think; blond—though this is a recent change—and blue-eyed like me. Until she had children, she was a modern dancer and she studied with Martha Graham. Now she has a graduate degree in Dance Therapy and has written a book and even teaches at Columbia, but she still isn't confident. Living with my father must be hard for her. He is hardly ever there, and when he is, he is usually thinking about something else.

I think my father would have liked a son. He says that's ridiculous, he prefers little girls. But I know what I feel. I've always felt it. That's why I wanted to be a boy for a while. Besides, my sister was such a perfect example of what a little girl should be that I could see right away it would be hopeless to compete. When I was five, I threw all the dolls out of my room forever and told everyone they had to give me horses instead. Now on my shelf I have sixty-eight horses. Bronze horses, china horses, Western horses, wooden horses. I don't *do* anything with them, except dust them when my mother nags me, but they are very comforting.

At first, I wanted to be a horse. Everybody laughed, though, whenever I'd say so. I didn't see what was so funny about answering that stupidest of all questions—"What do you want to be when you grow up?"—with a perfectly honest answer: "A horse." Even though I knew it wasn't possible, a horse was what I wanted to be. Eventually though, I had to give it up. That and sucking my thumb. Then I decided I wanted to be a boy. I wore dungarees all the time and followed little boys around to find out what they did so I could do it too. I had to pretend I wasn't afraid of course. That was the hard part.

Now that I'm thirteen, I am still confused. Part of me still wants to be a horse, to have a great neck to arch and long legs for galloping over the crests of mountains. And still, I want to be a boy, because, as everyone knows, boys have more freedom, and I like to do things for myself. But even though I have often pretended to be something else, the fact is that I am a girl. I can accept it. There are advantages, after all. Like not having to go into the army, for example. I am positive I wouldn't like it in the army. I mean, I always *hated* camp. Saluting the flag, Color War, rules. The reason I love my school is that it has hardly any rules. It's called Walden after the pond that Henry David Thoreau lived on all by himself. At Walden you are supposed to find out who you really are inside, the way Henry David Thoreau did.

My sister and I started going to Walden when she was six and I was three-and-a-half. I went into the nursery; she went into first grade. Then I skipped a year, which put me in the first grade and Diana in the third. Two years ago I skipped again, past sixth grade (Walden can get very chaotic) and turned up a year behind my sister, who had a tantrum. Now she believes that I am smarter than she is. Sometimes she believes it so strongly, she even convinces me.

Then I feel guilty. So I believe that she is more beautiful than I am—just to balance things out, because I like them better that way. That's why I want to learn to play the guitar, I guess. I love harmony.

2

LUCIA IS MY FAVORITE horse. I like her better than any horse I've ever ridden in my life, and I ride her once a week, before school when she is fresh.

During the coldest part of the winter, I ride her in the ring, taking her in figure eights around the pillars at a collected canter. It's like sitting on a wave that is always just about to break but never does.

Today, although I know my father wouldn't like it, I ask to take her out into the cold, clear air of deserted Central Park.

"Lucia's as spooky as a cat," Mr. Willson tells me in the office of the stable. "She hasn't been ridden since the day before yesterday."

"I can handle her," I assure him, even though I feel a fiery knot in my stomach.

"Well, watch out for baby carriages and blowing leaves, then. You know she'll bolt at anything."

"I know. She's never thrown me yet."

"She will." He sighs.

Soon I hear Lucia's hooves clattering a nervous tattoo on the concrete floor as she is being saddled. A moment later she's released onto the ramp. She ascends at full gallop, bursting out into the ring with white clouds of breath streaming before her. Through the office window, Mr. Willson is watching me mount. I am trying to sort out the reins while Lucia throws her head up and down and steps sideways. He opens the door and comes into the ring.

"You look like a jockey with your stirrups that short," he says.

"I like them short."

"I suppose you'll like flying over her head the next time she hears a baby carriage."

I rein her in, and we lengthen my stirrups. Then the stable door is sliding upward, and Lucia is bucking and backing up into the ring. I turn her head and trot her around. As we pass the street ramp, I bend her suddenly toward the sunlight. She hesitates a moment and then rushes down.

"You take it easy on that stupid mare . . .!" Mr. Willson calls as I sail past, and then I hear only the staccato rhythm of her hooves on the pavement. The echoes bounce off the sides of buildings into the hard light of early morning.

I know Lucia won't throw me because when I am mounted on her back, I am a part of her. I can react without having to think. She is so small, barely sixteen hands high, and delicate to the point of being perhaps a little skinny. Lucia's problem is nerves; she worries too much. She doesn't have enough self-confidence. Since that is my problem too, we get along. I know when to hold her back and when to let her have her way, when to let her buck and bolt and gallop off her energy. After an hour of tearing around the bridle path, we become almost relaxed.

Waiting for the light on Central Park West, Lucia champs at the bit and shifts her weight around. We are only a block away from Walden School, and anyone might see me. I put a little pressure on Lucia's ribs with my knees. Her neck arches and she does a little dance-step right in place, her hooves ringing for attention. I keep my gaze fixed between her ears, my hands light like feathers at the base of her mane. I am as cool as a statue.

Last fall I bought a sleeveless yellow sweater in the Junior Department at Bloomingdale's. In it, I imagined that my shapelessness was magically concealed. It looked, I told myself, as though the sweater didn't go in at the waist because it wasn't supposed to— rather than because I lacked a waist for it to go in at. I do not think anyone is fooled by my yellow sweater. The fact is, it hangs around the tops of my dungarees in lumpy folds.

Lately, I've been noticing the way the sweaters of the older girls mold themselves softly over their breasts and sweep around their hips. Then I look at the lumps of yellow Orlon bunched around my middle and feel absurd. Except for once a week. On horseback, I forget that my sweaters don't go in at the waist, forget that I have braces on my teeth and curly hair. I am the rider of Lucia: elegant and graceful as a song.

Although I walk as fast as I can from the stable on 89th Street and Amsterdam Avenue to Walden on the corner of 88th and Central Park West, I am late for Algebra. I hate Algebra. During class it feels as though a curtain has been drawn across my mind. I myself am in the wings, of course, working the pulley. Behind the curtain my thoughts and fantasies move about.

This is enjoyable, but, I ask myself, am I getting an education? If I were in a public school, I would definitely fail Algebra. I would not get into a good college. Everyone would be disappointed, and my life would be ruined. Happily, I go to Walden where it is practically impossible for anyone to fail anything.

To one side of me, Gloria, Jill, and Andra are circled around a pocket mirror and a tube of blue eyeshadow from Woolworth's. On the other side, Roger is turning his chair around to the usual card game in the back row.

"You guys want to shove over and deal The Kid in?" Roger asks.

As usual, nobody is paying the slightest attention to Algebra.

"Move over, dunghead."

"Eat me."

Laughter.

For months the boys have been playing tough GI's in a Korean war movie, waiting in the trenches.

"What IS Bob talking about today?" Jill asks about our math teacher.

"I don't know," Gloria shrugs. "I lost him at logarithms."

I say, "I lost him at square roots."

"We did those in October," Gloria needlessly reminds me.

"Well," I say, "it's only March."

"This year is going on forever," Andra mutters, deftly applying eyeshadow to her right eyelid.

"The worst part," I tell them, "is that I can't even do square roots."

"Sure you can," says Jill, passing me the eyeshadow. "They're just arithmetic."

"I can't do arithmetic," I inform her, smearing too much eyeshadow onto my lids. Removing the excess, my nose gets smudged. "I'm terrified of numbers," I say.

"What's terrifying about numbers? They're not even real," says Gloria, taking a bottle of perfume out of her purse.

"Just because they're abstract doesn't mean they aren't real. Anyway, flunking Algebra would be pretty real. My father would have a fit."

"Just how do you think you're going to flunk Algebra when Bob never gives anything lower than a C?"

"It's pathetic," I announce. "I have a totally blue nose."

One of the cardsharks wants to know what's for lunch.

"Your mother," Roger says.

"What do you think?" I ask Jill, about my eye-shadow.

"Maybe you'd better rub it in a little more."

"Hey, Dessauer," Roger calls in a stage whisper behind me. "Do you think Simon needs a bra?"

I rub in my eyeshadow, oblivious. Beneath my shirt I am conscious of the bra I do not need cutting into my flesh.

"Boys," I mutter to the girls, "are really just too much."

"What did you say?" Roger wants to know.

"I said," turning toward him, "that you boys are really schmucks."

"You see," he crows, "flat as a board!"

My early morning confidence has collapsed. Why do people go around hurting each other? I remember the first time I was ever deliberately attacked by another person. It was in the park. I was two-and-a-half, and I was playing with another two-and-a-half-year-old, a little girl with fiery red hair. Everything was going pretty well, I thought. We had pushed a lot of dirt into a pile and were sticking leaves and sticks into it when all of a sudden she reached over, casually took hold of my hair, and pulled hard. I was so insulted that I hid under a bush crying while my mother ran around frantically calling my name. It was a turning point in my life.

Sometimes I have to remind myself to be wary. I

say, remember: you never know when one of your perfectly innocent-looking playmates is going to reach over and pull your hair or tell you that you're flat-chested just to make you feel bad. Nobody can be trusted, I say, because everybody's crazy. Ask any psychoanalyst.

I wish I weren't flat-chested. Not that I would like a bust like Gloria's. In Chorus we are learning Mozart's *Te Deum*, and every time we sing the refrain, "Glorium Tu-um," someone in the tenor section adds on "BIGGUM!" and people laugh. I would not like having a bust so big that people commented about it, any better than I like having one so small that people make fun of it. Something in between is what I'm after, something not too big and not too small. Normal. I would do anything.

The bell is about to ring. Everybody is preparing to depart: shuffling papers, closing books, scraping chairs. No one pays any attention to Bob, who is not paying any attention to the impending exodus. He continues writing numbers and strange, squiggly signs on the blackboard. Bob is new this year. He will not be rehired. Everyone agrees that he is terrible. Not that he probably isn't a genius; he just can't communicate, that's all. He has skin the color of ashes, bags beneath his eyes, and dandruff on the shoulders of his V-neck sweaters. He is tired and going bald.

Bob was a mistake. They were going to replace him in the spring term, but they couldn't find anyone to replace him with. So he continues to masquerade as our Algebra teacher. Underneath the mask, though, he is miserable, a failure. That is why we can't look at him anymore or hear him. He's depressing.

The bell rings. The classroom door crashes open, and there is an explosion of din from the suddenly crowded halls. Everyone begins shoving and horsing around like a herd of lunatics.

When I look up, Roger is staring at me. Behind his thick lenses he has very large blue eyes. He is wondering if perhaps he went too far.

"You're a creep," I tell him.

"I apologize."

I love Roger. We've been in the same class together ever since we were three. Ten years has taught us what we can expect. I can expect to be teased; Roger can expect to be forgiven. We can expect to stay friends.

"I don't care," I tell him, "even if it's true."

"It isn't true. You're not as flat as a board. You're as voluptuous as Jane Russell."

"Don't be an idiot."

"I get hot pants just looking at you."

"Shut up, Roger," I giggle, butting my shoulder into him and blushing.

"Oooooo, baby," he says, putting his arm around me, "give me more . . ." He pretends to try and kiss my ever-evasive lips. I am squirming and laughing. His arm reaches farther around me. I feel his hand upon my back, my bra . . . SNAP!

"You . . . you *rat!*" I scream, flinging my arms across my suddenly liberated chest. "You'll pay for this!" I rush out the door and down the hall to the girls' bathroom where I can repair my ravaged underwear, if not my pride.

3

WHEN I WALK HOME from school along Central Park West, the air is filled with dampness and early dusk. The trees in the park are still wintery-bare.

Coming toward me, as I approach the awning of our apartment building, is a pale young man with a bony face sticking out of a turned-up collar. We reach the front door simultaneously. Our eyes meet for a second, and then I look away in a hurry: I realize he is a patient of my father's. It is curious, because I've never seen him before. I just know.

The doorman opens the door saying, "Hi, Winnie."

"Hi, Vernon," I say, "how are you?" But I keep my eyes on the strips of black rubber carpeting that are laid over the rugs in the lobby whenever it is going to rain.

Instead of turning to the north elevator or walking straight ahead to the west elevator, the young man and his bony face follow me to the east. I knew it, I think.

We have to wait an eternity for the elevator, which is stopping at nearly every floor, picking up passengers, delivering prescriptions and the afternoon *Post*. I stare at the arrow above the elevator and then at the floor. He stares at the floor and then at the arrow. Without noticing it, I have almost stopped breathing. What is more, my hands are clenched so tightly the nails are digging into my palms.

The elevator arrives. A bunch of people are crammed behind a baby carriage. Among them is the patient whose session has just ended. She smiles at me; I smile back. I have a funny feeling that she likes me, although I cannot explain why.

When we get into the elevator, the pale young man asks for "Ten, please," of course, and the elevator man whistles "Some Enchanted Evening," off-key, the whole way up. When we arrive, finally, I go to the door marked "Apartment," and he goes to the door marked, "Office: Ring Bell and Walk In."

He rings the bell.

He walks in.

I take a deep breath.

At dinner that night, I say, "Guess what, Father?"

No response. He is eating automatically, and his

eyes have that familiar, slightly glazed look that means that he is far away.

"Father? . . . Dr. Simon? . . . *Sir*?" I say.

"Yes?"

"Welcome back."

"Don't be silly," he says, "I heard you. You said, 'Guess what, Father?'"

"I rode up with a patient today."

"Really? What time?"

"Four-thirty."

"Ah."

"Male or female?" My sister wants to know.

"Male," I inform her, "around twenty."

"Cute?"

"Wait 'til you see him. He's just your type," I tell her. My father clears his throat. No one finds my joke funny.

"Does he go to college?" I ask.

My father pauses for a minute, as though finding his balance on a tightrope. "Yes," he says.

"What college?"

"You *know* he's not going to tell you that, you dummy," my sister says, "so why do you have to ask?"

Since I have no answer, I say, "Shut up, Diana."

"Winifred," (it is my mother) "eat your meat loaf."

"No," I say, feeling suddenly nasty, "I hate meat loaf."

"Don't be rude to your mother," my father says.

"I'm sorry," I say, without conviction.

"Well, I'm sorry you don't like my cooking," my mother says in a hurt voice.

"Can I be excused?" my sister wants to know.

"Anyway, I keep seeing him in the elevator after school," I tell my father.

"Maybe you'll fall in love with him and get married," Diana sneers.

"Maybe you'll fall into the Hudson River and drown." I smile back.

"Why do the two of you have to *fight* all the time?" my mother angrily inquires. "Please tell them not to fight at the table, Arthur."

"Don't fight at the table, girls. As soon as dinner is over, you can tear each other apart in private, okay?"

Later, I go down the hall to my father's office and find him sitting at his desk writing. It is a very orderly desk. Everything is clean and at right angles to everything else. The whole place is orderly. There is thick carpeting throughout, and sound-proofing tiles on the ceiling. The waiting room is connected on three sides to the apartment, and during the day, even with the sound-proofing, we are supposed to remember to be quiet. Since there is a buzzer in the kitchen that rings every time a patient enters the office, we are frequently reminded where we are. Whenever we forget, my father comes out and reminds us personally.

We all have to remember the rules of the game we are playing. One of the rules is that nobody can know anything about the patients except my father. Another, and even more important rule, is that the patients cannot know anything about anyone at all.

Entering, I say to him, "Could you look this over for spelling, Father?"

"Sure, Daughter."

"And don't *read* it, it stinks."

He glances down the page. "Immense is *i-m-m*, not *e-m*," he tells me, putting a little *x*, as is our custom, in the margin. "And you might try quoting more carefully; ye has only one *e*."

"Oh," I say innocently, "did I write it with two?"

"Both times."

My spelling is hopeless. I refuse to learn the rules.

"Winifred," (hopelessly) "there's an *e* before the *y* in Shelley. Why don't you look these things up if you're not sure of them?"

"That's just it. I am sure of them."

"God!" he says, opening his dictionary, "I start forgetting how to spell myself. . . . Ha, you got it right. Well, I think that's it. It looks very interesting."

"It's not."

"Why is that?"

"I couldn't concentrate on it. I've been having trouble concentrating lately."

"I've noticed."

"I haven't learned anything in Algebra since October. And I lost my wallet twice last week."

"What's on your mind, pussy-cat?"

"Lots of things."

"Such as?"

"I don't know."

"Oh, dear." He sighs. "It's so hard to be an adolescent. Believe me, sweetheart, I wouldn't be your age again for anything in the world."

I feel a rush of love for my father. He is so understanding, sensitive, intelligent, handsome.

"If I were president," I announce, "I'd declare adolescence illegal."

He laughs.

"I mean, it's sickening. You'd think they'd have discovered a drug to cure it by now."

"They have. It's slow-acting but effective. They call it aging."

"Oh, great."

"There's something else that usually helps, and that's talking to someone who's been through it. Do you think you'd like to go and talk to someone about what's on your mind?"

"You mean a psychoanalyst? Couldn't I just talk to you?"

"Of course, you can talk to me. But you're bound to have some problems that relate to me, and these are hard for us to talk about. Besides, I'm your father; I can't be objective about you the way someone else could be."

I'm not sure I want someone to be objective about me. Then he would judge me, criticize me. I don't think I want anyone who doesn't like me to know who I am. And what would I tell him, anyway? "I don't want to," I say.

"You know," he says, "everyone has the same sorts of problems. Yours aren't exactly unique."

I don't believe him. I am the only girl I know who ever got undressed with Tommy Collins. Thank God he has switched to another school. The thought of him torments me.

"What I mean is, everyone does things and thinks

things that make them feel guilty. Everyone makes mistakes, feels anxious, gets depressed and angry. We are all human beings caught in the human condition."

The Human Condition. I see it as the title of a book in many volumes. The pages would be onion-skin-thin and there would be thousands of them covered with minute print and bound in gold-tooled leather like my mother's collection of Shakespeare. I imagine myself reading down the slender columns and discovering what it's all about.

"That's really what you're in here doing all day," I say, suddenly inspired, "studying the human condition."

"I suppose so."

"And trying to change it."

"I wouldn't say that. I don't think it can be changed. Reality is reality after all. But it can be *experienced* as good or bad depending on whether people feel good or bad about themselves. I try to help people feel better about themselves."

I am so proud of my father. Could anyone be more noble, more understanding? "It's wonderful!" I say.

He looks embarrassed. "It's a job," he shrugs.

4

MY GUITAR TEACHER
wears orthopedic shoes and has a red crew cut
sprouting from his head that makes me think of
Howdy Doody. Also he is plump and doesn't always
bother to shave or sew up the holes that usually appear along the inside seams of his trousers. Nevertheless, he makes me feel nervous, silly in fact.

He is twenty-six years old, thirteen years older
than I am. He remembers Pearl Harbor, which happened before I was born.

Since September we have been meeting once a
week on the fourth floor of the Metropolitan Music
School, deserted except for a theory class two floors
down and sometimes the janitor mopping the marble stairs.

I always enter out of breath. Walter is playing jazz with his eyes closed at the piano. Since he would much rather play the piano for an hour than give me a guitar lesson, I don't want to disturb him. The only time he ever looks really happy is when he's playing jazz. But since my mother sends the Metropolitan Music School a check for twenty-five dollars every month, Walter must occasionally stop playing jazz and listen while I play, "Come All Ye Fair and Tender Maidens"—badly, because I am so nervous.

"It sounded better last week," he informs me when I'm through. "Didn't you practice it at all?"

"A little."

"And look at your fingernails," he says with a note of disgust, handing me his nail clippers.

"You're crazy," I tell him, "you made me cut them to the quick last week."

"They are," he says emphatically, "impossible."

I trim the nails on my left hand. Walter plays more jazz on the piano.

I don't know why I think some of the things I do. Really, I must be crazy. I am thinking: what if I were stuck here with Walter for the night? Suppose we were stranded on a desert island, or what if a bomb fell on New York City? Imagine if Walter seized me, suddenly, in his arms and . . . kissed me! . . . Raped me! How would I feel? Astonished, appalled, amazed. Thrilled and revolted. There is sweat on my palms.

"Why are you so restless today?" he asks me, through the music.

"I'm always restless," I tell him.

"Yes, but today you're even more restless." He

stops playing. "I'm going to show you a new pick, and I want you to watch carefully."

He takes out his Martin and plays a lilting, three-fingered pick. His hands are sort of pudgy, but they touch the strings with such assurance and grace it makes them look perfect, somehow, as though they were constructed for this very purpose, down to the freckles and funny little brown hairs.

"You got that?" he says.

"Huh?"

"What's the matter with you?"

I am shifting around in my chair, having become suddenly conscious of the conspicuous way the curve of my guitar cradles my right breast.

"Who? Me?" I say, clearing my throat.

"Pay attention then," he says. "Thumb, third finger; thumb, second finger; thumb-on-the-base-string, second finger; thumb on the A string. Unless its a D chord, of course. You got that?"

I play it back slowly, without the syncopation.

"Good. Practice that."

I practice it in the key of D. Walter joins in to show me where the emphasis goes and how the base runs fit in between the chords. We are playing music together. We look at each other and smile.

A gust of damp, bone-chilling wind blows me through the front door of the building and into the entryway. With a quick hello to Vernon, the doorman, who is struggling to close the door behind me, I dash into the lobby. Above the elevator the dial reads 10. Probably it is my father's 4:30 patient, I think, since it is just twenty minutes after five. The elevator descends, the door opens, and the same pale young man looks out at me, his face half-concealed by a turned-up collar. I look at the floor. That's two days in a row, I think. He must be pretty crazy. Boy, would I like to know what he talks about in there.

My grandmother, Sadie, is in the living room when I get home. She came to New York from the Ukraine in 1886 and remembers hiding in cellars from Cossacks on horseback. That was during the pogroms when she was very beautiful, she says. I am always studying her wrinkled face, trying to imagine it.

I'm the only person I know whose grandparents were divorced. It happened when my father was twenty. My grandmother says that my grandfather left her because he was irresponsible, and she has not talked to him for twenty-five years. But my sister says my grandfather left because my grandmother fell in love with someone else, a man named Henry who died. I think it's very sad, whatever the reason was.

Sadie is listening to classical music on WQXR and reading *The Guardian*, a socialist newspaper. Everyone on my father's side of the family is either a socialist or a communist except my father, who claims to be an anarchist. During the McCarthy hearings, the F.B.I. used to come snooping around, trying to get information about some of his patients, which of course my father wouldn't give them, because he hates the F.B.I. and everything it represents. And besides, no one is allowed to know anything about a doctor's patients, particularly if the doctor is a psychoanalyst. My father isn't even allowed to tell my mother about his patients, so he certainly wasn't going to tell the F.B.I.

My grandmother lives in Greenwich Village like the true radical that she is. Every Thursday she takes the subway uptown to have dinner with us. Usually she tries to help me with Algebra. Any math I've learned has been thanks to her efforts. After I kiss her with true affection on the cheek, she inquires about the Algebra quiz we studied for together last week.

"Oh," I say as casually as possible, "I flunked it."

"NO!" Her eyes widen with surprise.

"Yes. I don't think I got even one right answer."

"We'd better review it after dinner."

"Ugh."

"Guess what I have? An extra ticket for the opera. Would you like to go?"

"Gee, what night?" This is a game we play. No matter what night she mentions, I will say I'm busy. The fact is, I love my grandmother, but I hate going to the opera more than anything. I would rather study Algebra, and that's saying something.

"Friday," she informs me.

"Gosh, grandma, what a shame, I'm busy on Friday."

"You have a date?"

"Well, sort of."

"That's nice. You have a good time, dearie."

"You too, grandma."

"How could I help it? It's *Aida*. Do you remember *Aida*?"

It lasted for four straight hours. Four hours of peering over the rail of the very top tier of the Metropolitan Opera House. The stage looked about as big as a dime. Was it boring! Wow! I say, "How could I forget it?" but irony is wasted on my grandmother.

My mother comes in.

"Oh, hello, Sadie dear," she says, flashing the false smile that is reserved for my grandmother and one or two of my friends she particularly dislikes.

"Hello, Marge," my grandmother says, readjusting her glasses and smoothing the front of her large bodice in an automatic, anxious gesture.

"Dear," my mother says to me, "you'll have to get your paraphernalia out of the living room. Your father will be out soon."

"Sure," I say, "later."

If there is one thing my mother can't stand, it's me telling her I'll do it later.

"Now," she says. "Hang up your coat. And how many times must I ask you not to dump all your things in a heap?"

"Hi, Mom," I say. "Did you have a nice day?" Irony is not wasted on my mother.

"Just fine," she replies, looking straight at me. "How about a drink, Sadie?" She goes over to the bar, an empty martini glass in her hand.

"No, thank you."

"I'll have a coke, please."

"You will go inside this instant and put away your

35

things and wash your hands, and this is no time to have a coke, before dinner!"

I have to pass through Diana's room to get to my own. Usually I enter abruptly:

"HI!"

No response. She is on her windowsill, gazing into Central Park. Johnny Mathis is singing "The Twelfth of Never" on her record player.

"Hey," I say, "guess what?"

Silence.

"Grandma Sadie's here."

I can just see her profile silhouetted against the window; her domed forehead reminds me of the portraits of Dutch Masters in the Metropolitan Museum of Art, or maybe one of Botticelli's virgins.

"Aren't you going to say hello to her?"

"Aren't you going to get out of my room?"

"Boy!" I explode, "you and Mother are really something!"

If there's anything Diana can't stand, it's being told she has anything in common with Mother.

"You're asking for it," she threatens.

"Okay, okay. I'm just going into my room to put away my things."

"Then go."

Wow, I think, dumping everything onto my bed, is she crazy!

"What's the matter with you?" I ask, returning.

"I happen to be," she says, biting off the syllables, "in a bad mood."

"I can see that," I inform her.

36

"Then why don't you leave me *alone?*"

My father is at the bar fixing himself a drink and offering to pour Sadie a little glass of sherry, which she accepts.

After kissing me, he says he has a meeting at 8:45 and would I tell my mother he's in a hurry. I do, and she sends me to tell the maid to put the meat in right away and to invite my sister to the table.

Diana arrives after the invitation has been repeated by my father. My father is the only person in the family my sister respects.

"Is anything the matter?" my mother asks her.

"No."

"How is everything with you, Sadie?" my father asks.

"My arthritis is killing me."

"I'll give you a prescription."

"I want you to read an article in *The Guardian.*"

"Sadie," he says, "you know I don't have time to read that propaganda."

"It's not propaganda."

"All right, it's not propaganda." He sighs.

"Why do you say it's propaganda?" I ask.

"Because it distorts the truth," he tells me.

"If you would only *read* it, you'd understand," my grandmother insists.

"Understand what? That everything the Soviet Union does is perfect and everything the imperialist war-mongers do is terrible?"

"You know, Arthur, there *are* things they don't report in *The New York Times.*"

My mother says, "I thought we decided to do without politics."

"Someday you'll all see." My grandmother sighs. "I won't be around, of course, but the children will learn the truth."

"What truth?" I ask.

"Your grandmother firmly believes that the C.I.A. started the Hungarian revolution," my father says, in a tone that implies she might as well believe President Eisenhower plays squash.

My mother says: "Diana, why aren't you eating?"

My sister has been pushing the food around on her plate with a fork.

"In due time it will all come out," Sadie whispers.

"Arthur, you're the psychoanalyst, why isn't this child eating her dinner? Eat a little meat, darling," my mother tells her, "you'll feel better."

"Leave me alone," she replies.

"Leave her alone, dear," my father cautions.

"Don't tell me to leave her alone. What did *I* do?"

"May I be excused?" Diana says.

"No," my mother answers.

"Father?"

To change the subject, I announce, "I have a French test tomorrow and I don't know a thing."

"Then you'd better do some studying," my mother advises, "I haven't seen you open a book all week."

"That's not true!" I lie. "I've been studying like crazy!"

"Oh, yeah, sure," my sister mutters.

"How would you know? All you ever do is stare out the window."

"Shut up."

"Go to hell."

"That will do!" my father announces.

"I'd like to be *excused*," my sister repeats.

"How about some salad," my father interjects. "Would you like some salad, Sadie?"

"No, thank you, it doesn't agree with me," she says.

"Diana, have you painted any new pictures lately?" Sadie says.

"A couple," she answers with a bored sigh.

"You should *see* her new paintings," my father says enthusiastically. "She's almost a French Impressionist."

"Everyone always comments on the one over my mantel," Sadie says sweetly.

"Look, do we have to talk about this?" my sister demands. She does not like discussing her activities at the table. Other topics she does not like to discuss at the table include medical procedures—particularly injuries or operations—and animals.

"Guess what, Father?" I say, "we're going to dissect a chicken tomorrow in Biology."

"A chicken," says my father. "Is that so?"

"I am being *excused*!" my sister shouts, jumping up from the table. "I think you're perfectly vile, Winnie."

I amaze myself, really. Even though I really love people and want them to love me too, sometimes I act like the little red-head who pulled my hair in the sandbox. I know it's crazy, but I still do it.

"I just wish we could have an uninterrupted meal in this house once in a while," my mother complains. "Just one."

"Gee," my father says rising, "it's almost eight-thirty, I've got to run."

"I'll leave you *The Guardian*," Grandma assures him as he kisses her cheek.

Taking his briefcase from the hall table, he disappears out the door, and we are left, the three of us, to eat dessert and argue about whether I need a blue blazer or a crew-neck sweater to complete my spring wardrobe. My mother is strongly in favor of the blue blazer—so adorable with skirts—and I have to keep reminding her that I wouldn't be caught dead in one.

"Oh, well," she concludes, rising, "I suppose you'll lose whichever one you get inside of a week."

She is getting ready to leave because on Thursday nights she plays Canasta—for money—with some ladies in the building. Sadie and I are left to our brief Algebra review. Then I have to study French. Just before the elevator comes, Sadie implores me to read *The Guardian*, a special copy of which she has delivered to my room in a discreet brown paper bag.

5

I CANNOT READ *The Guardian* because it is so boring. Newspapers bore me to death, though I wouldn't admit it to most people.

The French test tomorrow is on two past tenses. I am supposed to be able to tell them apart. One is used for action that began in the past and is continuing into the present, and it's called the imperfect past, don't ask me why. The other one is used when whatever happened has finished happening. It's called the perfect past. *Par example* (it says in my text): *L'été dernier j'avais eté dans les Alpes Suisse.* This is false. Last summer I was high in the Rocky Mountains of Montana, and it was definitely the best part of my perfect past life.

For example: I rode a pure-bred quarter horse, jet black except for a single white stocking. The wrangler liked to tell a story about when Sugarfoot was a freshly gelded colt, and got turned out into a field of mares for the winter. The wrangler would lower his sky-blue eyes and bite at the inside of his cheek and clear his throat and then explain that Sugarfoot had been only half cut: when the horses were rounded up in the spring, every mare in the field was pregnant. Those warm weeks of stallion-hood remained branded into Sugarfoot's spirit. They also resulted in a dozen prize two-year-olds.

We were thirty-six girls, all from the East Coast, ranging in age from twelve to seventeen on the M-Lazy-V Ranch outside of Kalispell. We lived four to a cabin, and each cabin had its own cozy, pot-belly stove around which we played guitars and sang in the evenings. Far away, on another ranch, a hundred miles across the Rockies, forty boys of our age and origins were spending *their* summer. We had already spent four wild days with them on the train from New York. The plan was for them to visit our ranch in July and for us to visit them in August. This excited most of my friends. It did not excite me.

What did excite me was my horse. I spent hours with him, currying the dust out of his hide and brushing him to a gloss. Every day I'd comb through the knots tied by the wind in his flowing mane and check the bottoms of his feet for pebbles.

One hot afternoon in July, I turned Sugarfoot into the corral and went to work on my tack: cleaning the saddle and bridle, brushing out the saddle blanket. Everyone else had gone swimming, I think, or else they were napping in their bunk beds. The tack room of the barn was small, dark, cool, and very quiet. I sat for a while breathing in the tangy smell of pommeled saddles, the sweetness of fresh hay in the loft overhead, the strong, ripe odors rising through the window from the corral. Turning to my saddle, I saw Howdy, the wrangler, leaning against the door frame, his hat pushed back from his sunburned face, a shock of blond hair stuck to the wet of his forehead. I smiled. He asked me why I was always so happy. "I don't know," I said.

"You even look happy to see me," he said grinning, fully aware that everybody was always happy to see him.

He took a few steps into the crowded tack room and crooked an arm around the pommel of a saddle. He was wearing a Western shirt, of course. It was tan with white piping and snaps.

I'm not sure how it started. I only remember that when he started tickling me I went limp with laughter. When I was at his mercy, he grabbed a rope halter from off a nearby nail, and neatly laced my wrists and ankles together like they did when branding calves. This done, he slung me across his broad back and climbed the ladder into the loft.

There was sun radiating through a trapdoor in the peaked roof, and the great pile of golden hay into which he tossed me was dazzling. I would have liked just to lie there quietly in the hay, dizzy from the laughter, the radiance, the smell. But I was helpless.

Also I was naive. He leaned toward me, kneeling in the hay. I imagined he was going to continue with the tickling and giggled madly in anticipation. But he didn't tickle me. Astonished, I giggled harder. His face grew huge. The golden stubble of his beard looked remarkably like the hay, and his eyes were a bottomless blue. I didn't have any breath, otherwise I might have screamed. Since I was bound hand and foot, I could only thrash about.

He didn't take me seriously at first. Maybe I wasn't thrashing strenuously enough. Gradually, I got desperate though, frenzied. It suddenly felt like life and death were at stake, not just a kiss.

When he cut me loose, there were red marks on my wrists. Both of us were too embarrassed to say anything. After a minute I caught my breath, climbed down the ladder, and went swimming.

The drought, which had been parching pastures and drying up the creekbeds, moved into its third week. Our trails were tunnels of dust. Some cattle had broken through a fence in search of water. I had taken up the rear of a long column of horses on its way to round them up. Being high-strung and competitive, Sugarfoot did not like being held to the rear. But I kept him back anyway, enjoying the way his muscles tensed for the Western gait, called a lope, that he could do for miles. The dust from the horses ahead of us was so dense I couldn't see them, and my eyes were tearing as I peered ahead for branches to avoid and fallen trees to jump. Somehow I missed a fork in the trail. Suddenly the dust began to thin. Sugarfoot reared up, let out a piercing whinny, wheeled around, and dove into the brush. I was catapulted clean out of the saddle and went sailing headfirst and wide-eyed straight into the scrubby trunk of a ponderosa pine.

I remember thinking very calmly as I flew through the air that it was going to hurt. But I was wrong. There was a moment of absolutely nothing, and then I was lying at the base of the tree watching Sugarfoot's hoof descending on my outstretched leg. I shut my eyes. When I looked again, he was gone. His hoof had torn my jeans, but not even the skin was broken.

Since I wasn't really hurt, I don't know why I was crying, but that's how Howdy found me. He dismounted some distance away. He swung his left leg across his horse's neck, and sprang out of the saddle. He picked me up and held me quite still for a moment. Then he asked me if I was okay. "Sure," I said, "but where's Sugarfoot? Is he okay?"

"He's okay until I catch him. Then I think I just might break his fool neck," he answered.

"What do you mean?" I said. "Do you know what he did? Look—he came down here, right on my shinbone with his hoof. You see? My jeans are torn, but he didn't even break the skin."

"Of course not," Howdy replied. "What kind of a horse did you think he was anyway?"

"A great horse. I love him."

"Well, he's just a plain old, half-crazy quarter

horse, smart enough not to step down on another person," he said. "If you love him, that's your problem."

At night I shared a double-decker with a girl named Harriet, whose eyebrows grew together over her nose. I slept on top. Harriet rode a willful little buckskin relentlessly and carried her tack to the hitching post in a bow-legged imitation of the wranglers' swagger. Often, we would lie awake and Harriet would complain to me about life in general and God in particular. God was a disappointment, according to Harriet. She was very annoyed with Him for making her a girl. In case I didn't think that was bad enough, she happened to know it was going to get much, much worse.

"Oh, come on, Harriet," I said to her one night. "You'll probably be secretly glad."

"Are you kidding? I'm going to kill myself when it happens."

"Don't say that. It's probably going to happen nearly any minute."

"You shut up!" she hissed.

"And I bet deep down you'll like it."

"No, I won't!"

"Well, I will."

That week, doubled up with cramps, I wrote my mother a Strictly Private letter announcing my entry into the hallowed halls of Womanhood.

One afternoon in late July the boys arrived,

46

sprawled on the top of knapsacks in the back of a truck. One of them, a really cute one named Dan, who I'd played gin with on the train, came over to me right away and I showed him around the ranch. But later, after dinner, I began to be alarmed. We had assembled under the trees where the boys' sleeping bags were laid out, and all around me couples had formed, as though by wizardry in the moonlight. No matter how often I shifted my position, Dan was always at my elbow. Fortunately, somebody asked me if I'd play my guitar. I practically ran back to my cabin for it. Then I played it until the moon set, long after Dan had fallen safely asleep in his jacket and boots.

We saw the boys again when we arrived shivering under the tarpaulin of our own truck at their ranch. When the rain finally stopped, the August night was freezing, and the cabins to which the boys escorted us were icy. Dan clutched my hand. He was probably afraid I might dart off for my guitar any minute. The boys wanted to get drunk. The most potent thing they had, though, was vanilla extract, a bottle of which was passed around the room. Everyone took a ceremonial sip. Sitting with Dan in an upper bunk, my eyes grew gradually accustomed to the darkness. Couples were lying on the beds with their arms around each other. My friend Ann was lying stretched out against a boy whose name I didn't even know, but who was kissing her anyway, steadily on the lips. I couldn't take my eyes off them. Dan's breath was warm against my neck.

"What's the matter?" he whispered.

"What do you mean, what's the matter?" I said innocently.

"With you."

"Nothing."

"Then why don't you turn around?"

I turned, bending a knee between us. I was very nervous. "They're all making out," I observed.

"Yes. It's a lot of fun."

"Oh."

"Haven't you ever made out with anyone?"

"No."

"Oh, he said sadly. "Well, do you think you might like to try?"

"I don't think so," I said. "To tell you the truth, it scares me to death."

Dan's attempts to reassure me were unsuccessful. In fact, the more he rubbed my neck and blew into my ear, the more uncomfortable I got. By the end, we were both sorry I hadn't gone for my guitar.

The summer ended quickly after that. Before I knew it, we were heading for New York. I won't even try to describe my anguish. Leaving Montana tore me in two. I sat without moving for hours, afraid that if I stood up I might leap off the train. I think I fell asleep. When I woke up, the sun hung like fire over the mountains behind us. Ahead, it was already dark, and the earth was flattening out into the bleak Black Hills of South Dakota.

I got up to look for Dan. Eventually I found him in an upper berth, necking passionately with my friend Ann. I do not think they saw me. If they did, they didn't care. I stumbled down the corridor, almost sick from the shock. I thought again about leaping off the train. It was all so crazy. Dan was suddenly transformed into the most desirable male on earth—and I had cast him aside out of fear, lost him forever. I was an idiot, I felt, and yet I still couldn't imagine myself in Ann's position. My whole body resented the idea. It made me tense in every muscle.

I decided Harriet had been right. Not only was it difficult to be a girl, but it looked like it was going to get a lot worse.

6

SINCE LAST SUMMER IN Montana (it seems like six years ago instead of just six months), everything has changed. My father says it is because I am thirteen. He never fails to remind me he wouldn't be thirteen again for anything in the world.

At least he understands me.

I don't. Either I am racing around like a maniac, or else I feel lifeless as a stone. It is Friday, and even though I know I'm late for History, I can barely drag myself up the stairs. Relying heavily on the banister for support, I close my eyes and imagine I am Sisyphus, eternally rolling a boulder uphill.

"Ooops," I say, colliding with someone, "I'm sorry." I look up.

A senior named Donald Tressler, giantlike, powerful, is above me. He is grinning.

The sudden shock wave makes my knees buckle, and the light, for a moment, turns to darkness.

"I'm really sorry, excuse me," I sort of stutter.

"No." There is a gap between his two front teeth. His face bears the evidence of a long and futile war with acne. "You'll have to pay the penalty," he tells me.

We are alone on the stairs.

"Naturally," comes my careless reply.

Since he is a basketball player, he has quick responses. In the time it takes to blink, he has grabbed me and is pressing my body against his, forcing his lips onto mine and fighting his way through my teeth to penetrate my mouth with the sudden, alien heat of his tongue.

It is the weirdest sensation I've ever felt: a living thing inside my mouth. I am rigid with excitement, unable to move or breathe. When I start showing signs of suffocation, he stops, props me up against the banister, wipes the back of his hand across his lips, and continues casually downstairs.

That night I have a blind date. Diana is in a good mood for her. I have been given permission to get dressed in her room, for which I am duly thankful.

Laid out on her bed is my latest bargain from Bloomingdale's, which my sister maintains is the ugliest article of clothing she ever saw in her life. It is a salmon-colored wool sheath with short sleeves. It formerly had a little rhinestone brooch at the collar, which my mother persuaded me to remove.

"Guess what happened to me today," I say.

Diana is sitting on her windowsill in a shirt and underpants clipping her toenails. The parings are falling into the radiator grill.

"What?" she says.

"Maybe I'd better not say."

"Maybe you'd better since you brought it up."

"Don't tell anyone, okay?"

"Look, either tell me or get out of my room."

"Donald Tressler tongue-kissed me on the stairs."

"YIICH!"

"I knew I shouldn't have told you."

"That's disgusting! Was it?"

I *had* considered my initiation miraculous. "It was a little disgusting," I say.

"A *little* disgusting? His *tongue* in your *mouth*? What did you do?"

"Nothing."

"God, I bet you liked it, you little pig."

"No! I hated it!"

"You should have kicked him you-know-where. I would have."

"No, you wouldn't have."

"Well, I wouldn't have had to; you probably asked for it."

"I DID NOT!" I scream, because, of course, I know I did.

The doorbell rings. On my way to answer it, I am thinking about that airless afternoon during the drought when Howdy carried me giggling hysterically into the hay loft. I remember my frenzy when he tried to kiss me, how I strained at the rope, hurting my wrists but only tightening the knots.

What would I do now, I wonder? I have trouble thinking about it—about sex. I would rather think about horses, the way I did in Montana. But there are hardly any horses around here. I'd be better off in Montana, I'm sure of it. I would not be distracted by desire, would not waste my afternoons hanging around deserted classrooms, loitering on lonely landings courting casual caresses. I would not be insane.

I pause for a minute at the door, savoring a last flash of hope. Perhaps he will be strong and dangerously attractive. It is the danger, after all, that excites me. . . .

Unfortunately, my first impression is of pink skin, greasy hair and a tweed overcoat, such as my father might be expected to wear but wouldn't be caught dead in. He wears freshly polished black undertaker's shoes. I have an impulse to close the door.

"Hi!" he says. "I'm Louis Feinbaum. How're you?"

Beneath the overcoat is a pink and white pinstriped shirt, red and blue diagonally striped tie, and matching cuff links and tie tack. Inlaid mother-of-pearl, no less. His after-shave has a sad, sticky-sweet smell.

He starts talking immediately: "Wow," he says, "isn't this a big *place*. How many rooms you got?"

"Ten," I say, "counting my father's office."

"No kidding? What's your father do?"

"He's a psychoanalyst."

"No kidding! Does he psychoanalyze you?"

This question never fails to annoy me. "No," I say with a sigh, "he can't do it on his own family."

"No kidding? How come?"

"Because he couldn't be objective about us, and you've got to be objective," I repeat, not putting much into the explanation.

"Oh. I bet he does it anyway, though."

"What?"

"Psychoanalyze you."

"I'm his *daughter*. You can't psychoanalyze your own daughter."

"No kidding."

We take a taxi across town to a party filled with nobody I know, but even among strangers I'm embarrassed to be seen with Louis Feinbaum. It is intolerant of me, I know. If I had any self-confidence, I wouldn't care what other people thought. I wouldn't care, then, what Louis Feinbaum looked like, and the fact that he can only do the box step would probably amuse me. He is landing on my toes.

"Do you like the party?" he asks.

"Oh, sure, it's fine."

I would overlook his obvious faults and discover hidden reservoirs of talent and humor.

"I always like parties. Do you like parties?"

"Sure, when I'm in the mood."

Meanwhile, I'm in agony. If I think about it, the

smell of Louis Feinbaum's after-shave could make me want to vomit. Better to concentrate on that adorable boy over there with the sexy eyes—the one who looks just like Apollo. I mean, look at those eyes. What do you mean, look at them? I can't stop.

"Ouch!"

"I'm sorry. I lose track of my feet. I'm always losing track of my feet, which is funny. You know why?"

"Why?"

"My father's a chiropodist."

This Apollo boy has the sexiest eyes I've ever seen.

"A who?"

"A foot doctor, you know."

"Oh. Ha, ha."

The girl he's dancing with is madly in love with him, you can tell. He's tired of her though. She's pretty, but no personality. That's why he's so interested in me. Maybe he'll fall madly in love with me. I think I'll give him a little encouragement—a little smile. . . .

Louis says, "He says it's very interesting, but I don't know. I think I'd rather be a dentist."

A Frank Sinatra song ends and someone puts on a lindy. Louis and I retire to the food table. Roast beef sandwiches, ham and cheese, the usual.

We eat in silence.

After a while the boy with the sexy eyes appears and, reaching for a pickle, says hello.

Since Louis has his mouth full, I say, "Hi."

"John, this is Winnie," Louis mumbles.

"Who?"

I say, "Winnie"—and just so he won't forget—"as in Pooh."

After the party I want to say good-night to Louis in the safety of the lobby. It is not very nice of me, but what can I do? Kissing him good-night is out of the question, even if he has spent three dollars in taxi fares—even if he is, deep down, a generous, well-meaning person. He's still a creep.

When he asks if I will see him again sometime, I lie without hesitation.

"Next week is impossible, though," I explain, "I'm going to the opera with my grandmother."

The next day I decide to go riding, even though it is Saturday and will cost my father an extra dollar. He doesn't seem to mind. It's a beautiful day.

But when I get to the stable, I find Lucia is out. The manager tells me I should ride a new horse named Mr. Chips, who needs the exercise. He is so huge I have to mount using the block, and as soon as I am on his back, I can tell he doesn't trust me. The feeling is mutual.

On the bridle path I keep him first to a walk and then, by using all my strength, hold him to a trot. But he is tough-mouthed and headstrong. Soon my arms are trembling, more from anxiety than fatigue. There is a drumming of hooves behind us, and I look back to see a thin-necked bay, her ears flat against the top of her head, straining toward us in a desperate canter. Her rider is pounding her sides with his heels and lashing her rump with the reins. For a second, my heart is wrenched with pity and anger. Next I am in motion and everything is obliterated by fear. The bit firmly between his teeth, Mr. Chips lunges forward, and we are off. I have lost both stirrups. A moment later I have only one leg flung across the saddle. I'm hanging around his neck like a cowboy dodging bullets. Though I am terrified of falling, my alternative is hanging onto Mr. Chips as he gallops out of the park and into the traffic. I let go.

I hit the ground and roll over and over. Then I sit up.

Panic: I can't breathe. Disgust: my nose and mouth are filled with bridle path. I choke and spit and finally drag air and bridle path down into my lungs, sobbing. I am enshrouded in black soot. It is in my eyes, matting my hair, and stuffed into my pants, which have ripped up the rear seam as well as down one whole leg. I look up to see a mounted policeman approaching with Mr. Chips in tow. Though I know you're supposed to mount up after you fall off, I can't get up to do it. I am trembling all over. The base of my spine feels numb.

By the time I get home I am convinced I am seriously damaged. Perhaps, I think, going up in the elevator, I'll be paralyzed. Everyone will feel terrible, especially my sister who will remember all the hostile thoughts she has ever had about me and feel responsible.

"What *happened*?" she screams.

"I fell," I manage to sob through the remainder of bridle path still in my throat, "I think I broke my back."

"You bruised your sacroiliac," my father tells me. "That part of your back is called your sacroiliac."

"Is she going to be all right?" Diana, standing over my bed, wants to know.

"I'll give her some aspirin."

"Are you sure?" I ask.

"It'll make you feel better," Diana explains.

"No, I mean, are you sure that's all?" I am disappointed. At least I could have snapped a vertebra or two.

"It's very painful to bruise your sacroiliac," my father assures me.

"I know. Only . . . bruised. That's all? It isn't broken or anything?"

"No," he says, "only bruised."

I wake up stiff and depressed on Sunday morning to find out that everyone is going to Long Island to visit my grandfather, who has been sick all winter. I am sure he's not feeling half as terrible as I am. I tell them I can't go, my sacroiliac is killing me.

"What am I going to do with you, you're so accident-prone," my father says.

"Yeah," Diana mutters, "she's one big accident from start to finish."

I have an urge to say something rude in reply, but my parents are waiting in the doorway.

"Take it easy if you aren't feeling well," my father tells me.

"Try to do some studying, dear," my mother says.

"And stay out of my room," cautions Diana.

Just to spite her I go through her desk. Everything is in order: arranged, stacked, pigeonholed. Wrapped in tissue paper, way in the back, is her diary. I do not bother to read it. It would be more entertaining to study Algebra than read about the dumb things Ruthy said on the phone last night and how much my sister wants a new spring coat. Diana never writes anything personal in her diary. After all, someone might read it, and Diana likes to keep her personal life a secret. I'm no good at secrets. It's not that I mean to be deceitful, I just forget. According to Diana, this is one of my most annoying traits. I am not trustworthy, and she refuses to tell me anything interesting.

This doesn't stop me from offering up the choicest details of my inner life to her. I suppose I do it because I hope she will give me something in return, but she doesn't.

I leave the desk and move on to Diana's equally orderly bureau. Her new, wine-colored lamb's-wool sweater catches my eye. For an experiment, I exchange it for my yellow shirt, just for a minute. As I suspected, I look ravishing.

The phone rings.

I pick it up, saying, "Hi."

"Is this Winnie-the-Pooh?"

"Yes."

"How're you?"

"Fine."

"This is John Miller, do you remember me?"

Are you kidding? Apollo! I can't believe it. "Yes."

"Louis Feinbaum gave me your phone number. Would you like to take a walk a little later?"

I say yes, and we arrange a meeting. When: three o'clock. Where: in front of my house.

It is now one-thirty.

Don't get hysterical, I tell myself, but it is no use. I am feverish with excitement. I dash into the living room and begin doing leaps across the carpet. What will we do? What will I say? What will I *wear*? Racing into my sister's room, I throw open her closet. I have already borrowed her sweater. Dare I consider wearing her navy blue skirt as well? Too risky, I decide. Three *grands jetés* and I am in my room, ripping my own navy blue skirt off the hanger. Then, after tossing it onto my bed, I go careening into the bathroom like the true maniac that I am.

"Mother!" I yell, entering the apartment, "where *are* you?"

"In here, dear," muffled from the bedroom.

"I have got to tell you what just happened," I pant. "Are you ready for it? Mother, you've got to stop doing that so I can tell you."

She is plucking her eyebrows in a shaft of late afternoon sunlight.

"I can listen perfectly well, darling," she says. "Go ahead."

I am doubtful but can't contain myself. "You

won't believe this, but I met this *incredible* boy. He looks like Apollo, Mother, and he's brilliant!"

I pause, awaiting her response.

"How nice, dear," is all she says though.

"He's *fantastic*. You won't believe it."

"I'm sure I won't," she says, her gaze never leaving the mirror.

"And you know what?"

"What?"

"He's a senior."

She looks up, arching her eyebrows: "How about hanging up your new coat?"

"What's the matter with you?" I ask.

"Nothing. I'm delighted. What's his name?"

"John"—I sigh, forgetting my mother—"Miller. Couldn't you *just*?"

"Just what?"

"DIE."

"Winifred! What about your coat?"

"Guess what his father does?"

"I give up."

"He's a writer! And not only that, he's a *blacklisted* writer!"

"Wonderful. Where does he go to school?"

"Riverdale. He's a genius, Mother, I'm not kidding, and I'm absolutely positive he liked me."

"I'm absolutely positive he liked you too, dear, but please don't get yourself all worked up over nothing. I hate to see you disappointed."

Will somebody please tell me why my mother can't be a little optimistic sometimes? "This is what you will not believe," I tell her. "Are you ready? Guess what he wants to be?"

"What?"

"A PSYCHOANALYST! Isn't that the absolute and total END?"

"Yes," she says, "it is."

A week later I am gazing at the portrait of Apollo in my mythology book while the class is learning French.

"*Qu'est-ce que vous faites*, Weenie?" Mme. Lascot is asking, large circles of sweat expanding under the arms of her white blouse.

"Oh, *rien, rien. Excusez-moi.*"

"*Bien. Alors, traduisez, s'il vous plaît, le prochain passage.*"

"Um, the boy. . ."

"The boy*s. Les garçons!*"

"Oh, of course. Let's see . . . the boys and the girls went all in to buy."

"No! Janette, *ma cherie, essayez-vous.*"

"All the boys and girls went to buy some."

"*Oui! Voilà. Maintenent, écrivez, s'il-vous-plaît.*"

I watch as Madame shapes—precisely, almost angrily—the words of the dictation with her elasticized, scarlet mouth. As the circles of perspiration widen to frame each of her enormous bosoms, I decide that it would be impossible to learn French from someone so grotesque. And, just to prove my point, I hand in a hastily scribbled list of disagreeing articles and unconjugated verbs.

Outside an icy rain is falling. Everyone is irritable,

pushing in the halls, jamming the stairway down to the lunchroom.

"It's lucky I'm not even hungry," I say to Janet, as we stand gazing at the platter of pinkish macaroni and cheese on the food table. We each take half-a-dozen slices of white bread and two cartons of milk to an empty table in the rear.

"I'll never make it through this day," I tell her when we sit down. "I've given up hope. If he hasn't called by now, he never will."

"I'm sure he'll call you tonight," she says with no conviction.

"You were sure he'd call me last night."

She shrugs.

"It's *depressing*," I complain.

"Boys are jerks," she says.

I look at Janet, who of all of us is the most beautiful. Her face is perfect enough for Hollywood. Last year, in fact, she had a screen test for the lead in a Hollywood movie, *The Diary of Anne Frank*. I agreed to go along to Hollywood as her companion —on the condition that she fix me up with Marlon Brando, whose slave, I admit, I would gladly be. In the end, she didn't get the part.

"Hasn't David Ruben called you?" I ask.

She shakes her head.

We sigh.

"How did you do on the dictation?" It is Mark, the cardshark, macaroni slopping over the side of his plate, sitting down opposite us.

"Don't mention it," I tell him, "I thought it was impossible."

"Oh," he says, "I thought it was easy."

63

"Here he is, folks!" Roger announces himself, setting an equally repulsive portion down next to Mark's. "I bet I got an A on that dictation. Boy, was it a cinch. Hey, Mitchell!" he shouts through the din, "I bet I did better on that quiz than you!"

"Oh, yeah?" comes the reply. "You want to bet?"

"How much?"

"A quarter."

"Too much."

"Too much, your mother. A quarter says I got at least an A minus."

"God, the conceit!" I say to Janet.

"You'd be conceited, too, if you were as brilliant as me."

"As *I*, schmuck," Mark says with a stuffed mouth.

"Don't be silly, Mark," Janet tells them. "When you're that brilliant, you don't have to worry about trivialities like grammar."

"So true," Roger says, seizing one of the four milk containers he has stacked in front of him.

"If there's one thing I can't stand," says Jill, tilting her chair back from the adjacent table, "it's fat, conceited boys."

"Yeah," Roger says, as though the remark were addressed to someone else. "How's your ass, Jill?"

"None of your fat business."

"*You*," he says, "are cruisin for a bruisin."

Beyond the windows of the basement level lunchroom, I can see the pavement lashed by sheets of rain. Inside, the air is steamy, laden with the smells of macaroni and spilled milk; heavy with remarks that make me think of John Miller and how, once again, I have set myself up to be hurt. I gather up my breadcrusts and crumpled milk cartons, dump them in the can at the door, and head for the stairs. Depressed.

In the lobby a girl who's going steady with a boy at Riverdale says, "I saw a friend of yours in the park yesterday."

"You did?" I am instantly breathless—expecting a message.

"You'll never guess who he was with. Rachel Toby."

Rachel Toby doesn't even go to Walden, but everyone knows who she is. That's because Rachel Toby has, according to the latest survey, the Best Breasts on the Upper West Side.

I could kill myself.

7

DIANA HAS NOT BEEN in her right mind all week. Today she has taken to calling me "Pooh." Not only that, she is singing in the bathtub, and when her phone rings, she asks *me* to answer it.

It is a boy with the ridiculous name of Randy Robbin. I inform Diana, who tears like a shot from the bathroom, clutching a towel around her, and dripping a stream of water onto the carpet. With her hand over the mouthpiece, she gestures me out of her room.

My mother is in the living room reading a book about modern dance. I wonder what it has to say about her, and she says, "Don't be ridiculous, darling, I wasn't famous."

66

"Maybe you will be," I say, imagining that if a picture of our family should suddenly appear on the front page of the *Times*, John Miller—who hasn't called in twelve days—would certainly be sorry. "Maybe Father will be famous," I muse. "I know! President Eisenhower will appoint him head of something, Head of the Head-Shrinkers, ha, ha. Then he'll win the Nobel Prize."

My mother says, "I think everything is fine the way it is."

"I don't."

The phone rings.

"Excuse me, dear," she says, and hurries into her bedroom.

When I reenter my sister's room, most of her wardrobe is on her bed. In a bra, a half-slip, and high heels, she is pulling a green wool dress over her head.

"Could you zip me up?" she pleads.

I do.

"What do you think?"

"It's great. I love that dress." She looks, I think, beautiful. Her hair has begun to grow out. It catches the light now and glows tawny-red like a cat's.

"I hate it," she says. "Unzip me."

"You're crazy," I tell her, obeying.

"Oh, God!" She steps out of the dress and flings it onto a chair. "What am I going to *wear*!?"

"How about the paisley?"

"Don't be silly. That looks vile on me."

"Then can I have it?"

"No. Come on, Winnie, help me or get out of my room. I have a date."

"Ah, hah. A date, you say. With whom?"

"Randy Robbin."

"All right. Now, here's the important one: when?"

"Friday night, the day after tomorrow."

"A date. Randy Robbin. Friday. I've got it!—The mustard jumper."

"You *must* be kidding. You don't think it makes me look fat?"

"No."

"Well, that just proves it."

"What?"

"That you want me to look ugly and you are a selfish little pig. Now, will you please get out?"

On Friday Randy Robbin comes right on time. I have to answer the door because Diana does not receive her dates personally, and my parents are out. Suave is the word for Randy. He reminds me of my mother's sealskin coat: dark and rich and buttery-smooth. He says all the right things and smiles incessantly. Together—my sister in a new, empire dress from Bonwit Teller—they look ravishing. When they have gone, I feel depressed.

With nobody around, I play the guitar, think about John, and feel sorry for myself:

> "Come all ye fair and tender maidens
> Take a warnin' how you court your men.
> They're like a star on a summer's mornin'
> First they appear and then they're gone."

When the doorbell rings, I cannot imagine who it is.

Mike Josephs and Bob Abrams, two classmates of my sister's, are waiting in the hall. "Hi," I say, thrilled to see them, "come in."

They do, dumping their coats on a chair.

Naturally, they want to know if Diana's home. I apologize and say she's out on a date.

Mike says, "That's too bad. We wanted to take her to a party, didn't you, Bob?"

"Yeah, Mike, you sure did."

"Well"—Mike sighs, walking toward the bar—"it's really a shame you won't have a date."

"Would you like a coke or something?" I ask.

"Yes," he says, "with plenty of ice."

I have to go into the kitchen to get some. When I return, Bob is sitting on the couch with his feet up on the coffee table, and Mike is fishing two Lucky Strikes out of a pack in his pocket. Both are wearing jeans and v-neck sweaters over ivy-league shirts. Mike is, I suppose, the cuter of the two. He has curly blondish hair and a slightly turned-up nose. Bob has dark, very short hair and is a little heavy. It doesn't matter to me though. His long, aquiline nose and cruel eyebrows interest me.

"There must be *someone*," Mike is saying, "because we have to meet Nancy there in fifteen minutes."

"Well, maybe you'd better go alone," Bob suggests, his face and voice expressionless.

I am standing with the cokes, waiting for them to light their cigarettes, hardly daring to breathe.

"What about Diana's little sister?" Mike wonders, settling back in his chair.

"What about her?" Bob inquires.

"Why not take her?"

Bob's eyes narrow. He blows several smoke rings in my direction. "I don't know," he says. "Why not?"

Since there is no reason not to, they decide to take me if I can be ready in five minutes, which I can and am.

We walk down 86th Street, and though a stiff wind from the Hudson River is blowing in our faces, I do not feel the cold. What if John Miller was there? What would he think if he saw me with Bob Abrams?

When we enter the lobby of 810 West End Avenue, Nancy Blaire, a thin, pale, waxen-haired sophomore from the Birch Wathen School, is waiting. Nobody says anything in the elevator. Getting off, Mike puts his arm around Nancy, goes with her to the door of 7A, and rings the bell. I stand a little behind and a little to one side of Bob feeling suddenly conspicuous. I shouldn't have come. I am awkward, unattractive. It is obvious that Bob doesn't want to be seen with me. If John is here, I'll commit suicide.

When we go inside, I realize there is nothing to worry about.

Nobody could see us if they tried.

And nobody's trying.

If Diana came to this party (which is unlikely because she thinks Bob Abrams is a pig), she wouldn't have stayed for a minute.

I suppose she would think I was a pig, too, for

sitting here on the floor in the dark and drinking beer, which I can't even stand the taste of. Well, I don't care. Diana is a prude, and everyone knows that prudes have no fun.

Here people are having fun. Some of them are dancing, for example, but nobody gets in anybody else's way. That's because nobody is moving. At least, nobody's feet are moving.

I am still too nervous to talk. I don't want to say the wrong thing, after all. So I sit next to Bob on the floor, drinking my beer, trying to relax. It's not easy. I'm not sure what position I ought to put myself in, and every one I try feels unnatural. The most important thing, I decide, is to hide my discomfort from Bob because it would only make him dislike me even more than he obviously does already (if that is possible). He's so cool. I wish he'd like me. (It would serve John right.)

"You don't look very comfortable," he says.

"Oh, I'm okay."

"Come here," he orders, taking hold of my arm to lean me up against the wall.

I feel a flash of fear. Thrilled, I let my shoulder rest against his arm.

There is nothing wrong with it, I tell myself, I've known Bob Abrams all my life. He's always been in Diana's class. And I've always thought of him as a kind of cousin, except that none of my cousins are nearly as cool as Bob Abrams.

Now he is sliding his arm behind my back in a way that suggests I'm not supposed to notice. I take another sip of beer, which has gotten warm and tastes worse than ever. It has made me a little light in the head. Bob's hand creeping around behind me feels ridiculous, but I cannot laugh no matter what. I better not move, either, or think about how he is rubbing my arm. *I'm* not doing anything wrong. Diana wouldn't like it though. She'd never let Bob Abrams rub her arm ... or pull her closer to him ... or let him kiss her like this. But what should I do? If I didn't let him, he'd think I didn't like him. It would make him feel bad. Oh, God, why have I put my arms around him? Now he's lowering me to the floor—what if somebody *sees*?

"Wait a second," I gasp.

He releases me instantly. "Yes?"

I straighten out my pleated skirt, tuck in my sweater, pull my socks up, and clear my throat. "Okay," I say, "I'm all right."

"Are you positive?" he asks, jabbing me in the ribs.

"Ow! Are you crazy?"

He fakes a punch to my left shoulder and, when I react, pokes me in the ribs again.

"Cut it out," I tell him.

"Don't you like it?"

"NO!" I say, as he tickles my other side, "I don't."

"I thought you did."

"Well, you were wrong," I insist, punching at him, "so stop it."

In one move he has wrestled me to the carpet again and is holding my arms behind my back. "What's the magic word?" he wants to know.

"Please." I do not hesitate to beg.

He lets my arms go but keeps me where I am. We

stare past each other for a minute, then he resumes kissing me.

It doesn't matter. Everybody is too engrossed in doing the same thing to notice. Still, I don't feel exactly right about it. I think I ought to offer some resistance, just so he won't get the idea that I'm used to doing this and talk about how fast I am in the locker room at school. Maybe he really likes me, though. He doesn't *seem* to, but you never know, I mean, he's making out with me, isn't he? I wish he'd say something instead of blowing in my ear. He could tell me how he feels, how he's loved me all his life and wants me to go steady with him . . . marry him someday. I'd accept of course . . . he'd give me an ankle-bracelet, which I would have to hide from my mother because I know she thinks they're cheap.

Suddenly, the room is flooded with light. We sit up and blink through the glare at a dozen couples frozen in various attitudes of surprise. In the doorway, a small gray-haired man is standing with a smaller, red-haired, overweight woman, obviously his wife.

Since the parents belong to a boy from Franklin who doesn't even know me, it's ridiculous to be so frightened. But I am. I'm terrified of authority, even when it is represented comically: by a little man with a bow tie and his littler, fat wife. Sometimes I can almost pity myself for being so pathetic. Sighing, I agree with Bob that we should leave.

Even with the wind at our back I am freezing. He walks a little ahead of me, the way the men do in Japan. What if we were in Japan and I was taking little running steps on tiny feet with eyes fixed on the hem of my husband's kimono, an inch or two above the ground?

As soon as we get to my corner, Bob stops beneath the impersonal light of a streetlamp to which a police call box has lately been attached. He says, "See you Monday," and I nod, hoping he will kiss me good-night. He doesn't.

8

OUR ENGLISH TEACHER
informs us that it was exactly noon when Actaeon
left his hunting companions and bloodied hounds
to rest after their morning of running game in the
forest. Noon, he explains, is the moment when the
sun completes its powerful ascent and balances above
the earth before its plunge to night and death.

With no apparent purpose, he says, Actaeon wan-
dered from the familiar paths into the depths of the
unknown wood. Here, he came upon a wall of cy-
presses and tangled vines and curiously cut his way
through to a large, sunlit grotto within.

Watered by a stream that widened into a pool,
this was a sacred place: a goddess's grove. And in it
Artemis was bathing, naked, among her nymphs.

A shriek of horror arose as the nymphs all rushed to hide the goddess from the intruder's sight. But Artemis towered above them all, and so Actaeon stood and stared. Her quiver and bow were out of reach upon the bank, but taking the only thing at hand—some water—the goddess threw it angrily into Actaeon's face, and from his once-human head antlers began to sprout, and his neck grew long and hairy, and his arms became legs, and his hands and feet turned into cloven hooves, and it was then that his own hounds caught the scent of a great stag in the forest.

Artemis watched while Actaeon's own companions made the kill, then went her way.

The boys think Artemis is a bitch. Actaeon was only wandering along, they say, he didn't mean any harm. But I say, he should have known better than to hack his way so brutishly through the wall of under-brush, the vines, the leaves—as though they were as dead as the animals he and his dogs had spent the morning killing. Actaeon, after all, was in Artemis' sacred realm. He knew the rules, but he broke them: he asked for it.

After school, Janet and I hang around waiting for a divinely inspired punishment suitable for Bob Abrams, the cad. We don't want to harm him physically, we decide; a truly humiliating experience would satisfy our lust for revenge. My favorite leaves him naked in the middle of Times Square, just as we come walking by, surrounded by photographers, and flanked by our new boyfriends, Marlon Brando and either Cary Grant or Anthony Perkins —Janet can't make up her mind.

I say Anthony Perkins is queer, but she doesn't think so. I don't press the point. James Dean's death was a terrible blow from which she has yet to recover. Her crush on James Dean started in the beginning of *East of Eden* when he kept banging his head against the tree so hard it made Julie Harris cry. Janet cried too, straight through the entire movie, which is not unusual for her. I could sympathize, but I'm not that emotional myself. Except when it comes to Marlon Brando. Then I die.

Walking home that afternoon, I am thinking that the goddess Artemis had the right idea: chastity. Just then, I think I see my father's 4:30 patient, bundled up as usual, entering our building. I turn around, walk back to the corner and then slowly up the block again. When I get to the lobby, the elevator doors are just closing.

Upstairs I find my sister in the living room and tell her I've decided to become a nun.

Right away I don't like her attitude. "You can't," she says flatly.

Her self-assurance infuriates me. "Why not?" I want to know.

"There are no Jewish nuns."

"So? I'll be the first."

"You're an idiot, and you know what grandma Sonia would do? Kill herself."

"Oh, that's a piece of crap," I tell her nastily.

"Go ahead, talk like a pig. Aren't you intelligent enough to express yourself without having to swear all the time?"

"Go to hell."

"See? You don't even realize how disgusting it is when you talk that way." I can tell from her tone of voice that she is enjoying her lecture. "What you have to do is learn how to *control* yourself," she says. "That is, if you want people to have any respect for you. No one has any respect for fast, foul-mouthed girls, you know."

She is asking for it, I think. "I am *not*!" I shout very loudly.

"Listen," she says, "I'm giving you some good advice. Why do you think it is that John Miller never even called you back?"

This is too much. "You're a bitch!" I shout.

"You're a slut."

That's it, I think, hurling my books to the floor and advancing toward her, still in my coat.

"Get away from me," she says, rising.

I grit my teeth. I can't decide whether to punch or strangle her.

"If you don't leave me alone," she says, holding her ground now, "I'll get you where it really hurts."

"Oh, yeah?" I crouch to protect my chest—I know she means it. "Let's see you try," I challenge.

"I'm not going to hit you first, you little monster. Now get out of my *way*!" As she lunges past me, I give her an almost unintentional shove. She is thrown off balance, turns to sock me back, and stubs her toe against the marble coffee table. The pain,

I can see, is severe enough to drive her to extremes; I wouldn't stand a chance against her now. I better get out while the getting's good.

I wheel around and tear out of the room. She follows, screaming, but I round the corner into the bathroom just in time, slam the door and, just as she begins pounding on the other side, manage to turn the key in the lock.

Diana is yelling that her toe is bleeding and I better let her in right away if I know what's good for me. But I'm too smart to fall for that. Besides, she can go wash her bloody toe off in the kitchen, the rat. There is an abrupt silence now beyond the door; another one of her tricks which I'm not falling for. Then, suddenly, there is a sharp rapping. "Go to hell!" I shout.

"Unlock that door and come out here *immediately!*" It is—(oh, my God!) my father.

The first thing I notice when I open the door is the pink of my father's face. It is not a color I usually associate with him. I might think he was suffocating or something, except that I can hear him breathing all the way over here. He is practically too angry to talk, and to tell the truth, I wish he wouldn't try. I don't want him to ask us how we could fight in the living room during his office hours. This is just what he wants to know, of course. "What is *wrong* with the two of you?!" he demands.

Diana and I have been struck dumb. We cannot even look in his direction.

"Do you think this is some kind of a *joke* or something? Can't you two get it through your heads that there are higher priorities than your incessant squabbling? There was a *patient* in the waiting room during all that, a *patient* listening to you, DO YOU UNDERSTAND?"

I nod my head automatically, but keep my eyes on the floor.

"I won't have it," he announces, "and I'm not kidding." Then he turns on his heel and marches from the room.

We are in agony. I steal a glance at Diana, who is standing rigidly by the window. "That was all your fault," she hisses.

"It was *your* fault," I growl back.

"Shut up," she says, just as the door flies open and my mother, in a rage, enters the room.

"Are the two of you out of your minds?" she demands.

I do not reply. Diana, though, can be heard to mutter something unintelligible beneath her breath.

"What?" My mother wants to know.

"Nothing."

"I do not understand how two little girls who have *everything* could be so ungrateful," she announces.

I sigh quietly. Diana can be heard muttering again, something like, "Oh, can it, Mother."

"I don't want any smart talk from you, young lady," my mother says, "or both of you are going to be punished but good!"

This time Diana's response is audible: "Oh, leave me alone," she says.

"You are not to give any more orders around here," my mother snaps. "Just who do you think you are?"

"Who do you think *you* are?" my sister sneers.

"Diana" I exclaim, "cut it out!" She is really asking for it this time. What is she, crazy or something?

"I will not have you being fresh," my mother shouts. "Do you hear me?"

"Yes!" I yell before my sister can say anything, "we hear you and we won't be fresh and we won't fight any more and we're sorry!"

"Now," Diana says, "leave us alone."

My mother's jaw tightens. "You are ruining your father's career!" she says dramatically. "You are so spoiled and self-centered that you can't even consider your poor father who exhausts himself working all day and all night to pay for your educations and all your things—your clothes"—here she picks up a blouse from my sister's chair and waves it in the air—"which you can't even put *away* for God's sake!"

"Don't touch my things!" Diana hisses.

"Shhh," I say to her, "be quiet."

"Because," my mother continues, "you're mean and spiteful and selfish and I don't know what I'm going to *do* with you!"

"Then why don't you just leave us alone?" my sister says again.

There is a deadly pause. My mother is fighting for self-control. "I'll leave you alone," she announces coldly, and throwing the blouse on the floor, she strides out of the room, slamming the door behind her.

For a long moment we do not move or speak. I feel something like a tickling deep inside my stomach for which I have no name. It seems to enlarge each time I take a breath, like a balloon, I think, but of bubble gum—pink and sugary, and wobbling on the verge of a sticky collapse. I take a look at Diana, she looks back at me.

The next moment we are in convulsions.

It is like dissolving into a mist; my life passes before my eyes and it is a miracle of humor, a gigantic joke.

We are gasping for breath, moaning.

"Do you remember," she says, "when I was five and you were three and we"—here she is forced to break off—"and we"—again, she's overwhelmed—"sprinkled Johnson's Baby Powder all over the living room because it hadn't snowed?" She is giggling uncontrollably, seeing it like a movie. "I made you do it." She somehow manages to continue. "I convinced you that Mother and Father"—she breaks down again—"Mother and Father"—giggle, choke—"would like it!"

Naturally, they didn't.

"I wonder why I did that," my sister says catching her breath. "I mean, I must have known they'd be furious. I think I did it to get back at them for something, probably for having you."

"You resented me," I say.

"You're not kidding."

"All my life, you resented me. But I love you."

"I love you too—sometimes."

9

ACCORDING TO *The New York Times*, a tornado ripped through downtown Dallas yesterday. Although it is April, the worst blizzard ever is raging in the mountain states, Montana among them. Nikita Khrushchev is in New York, and Vice-President Nixon's back from Africa. Diana enters the den with four oranges. "So?" she says. "What's on?"

Turning to the TV listings on the last page, I say, " 'The Big Surprise'—a stupid quiz program—or a show about Marines."

"God!" she says. "Then what?"

" 'Private Secretary,' 'Wyatt Earp,' 'The Jane Wyman Show,' or hockey."

"Private Secretary."

"Wyatt Earp."

"NO!"

"How about "Gunga Din" on the Million Dollar Movie starring Cary Grant and Joan Fontaine?"

The phone rings in my parents' room.

"You get it," I say.

"No, you."

"I got it last time."

"Well, *I* got the oranges."

"Hello?" I say into the receiver.

"Hi."

Silence, except for a loud pounding in my ears.

"How're you?"

It is—I am fainting—John Miller.

"Fine, how're you?"

"Fine."

In the pause I can hear the crosstown bus heading into Central Park.

"What have you been doing?"

Wishing you'd call, I think. "Nothing," I say. "I mean, nothing unusual. How about you?"

"I've been doing a lot of reading."

"Really?"

"And thinking about you."

"You have?" (I could faint, I swear it.)

"I wanted to tell you why I didn't call, okay? It wasn't that I didn't like you. It was that I *did* like you. Then I found out you were only thirteen."

I don't know what to say, and I am so weak in the knees it's hard to stand up. I carry the phone over to the windowsill and sit down.

"Are you still there?"

"Yup."

"How'd you get to be a freshman at thirteen?"

"I was put ahead in kindergarten and I skipped the sixth grade," I tell him, "because I was so mature for my age. I'm still mature for my age."

"I know," he says, "but couldn't you be just as mature for fifteen, or even fourteen? Do you have to be thirteen? I mean, it's just so close to *twelve*."

"It's awful," I admit, giddy now with elation, "I can't tell you how embarrassing it is."

"I can imagine," he says, and I know that he's smiling. "Are you free on Friday?"

"Yes."

"Everyone is going to say I'm robbing the cradle, you know."

"So what," I say recklessly, "they won't know what fun it is."

He laughs. "How about eight o'clock?"

I love you, I think. "Eight," I say, "yes, good night."

By 7:30 on Friday I am insane. Having been completely ready for an hour, I am now pacing around my sister's room, pleading desperately: "I'll give you anything you want. I'll never come into your room again as long as I live. You can wear *anything* of mine."

"No."

"How can you be so horrible? All I'm asking is just stay in your room 'til we've gone. Why won't you?"

"Because," she says, calmly unbuttoning her shirt, "it's insane."

"What are you *doing*?" I shout, "You're not changing your *clothes* are you?" This is it, I think. "What do I have to do, fall at your feet?"

"No, get a grip on yourself."

Horrified, I watch as she takes the wine-colored lamb's-wool sweater from her drawer and slips it on. This is the scene that is playing on my mind:

> (*Curtain. The Simons' living room on Friday in the late spring of 1957. Doorbell.* WINIFRED *rushes across stage to answer the door, looking flat-chested in a shirtwaist dress. Enter* JOHN *wearing an ivy-league air of sophistication.*)
>
> WINIFRED: Hi!
>
> JOHN: (*taken aback by her enthusiasm*) Hello. (*There is an awkward pause.*)
>
> WINIFRED: (*breathlessly*) Come in, have a seat. Would you like something to drink? There's no one here!
>
> (*Just then,* DIANA *enters, looking like a movie star in tight jeans and a wine-red sweater.*)
>
> DIANA: Oh, hello, there.
>
> JOHN: (*rising so rapidly he might have been stuck with a pin*) Hello there.
>
> WINIFRED: (*horrified*) I mean, except my sister. John, this is Diana. Diana, this is John.
>
> (JOHN *crosses to center stage and takes* DIANA'S *hand.*)
>
> DIANA: Winnie's talked *so much* about you.
>
> (WINIFRED *wilts visibly.*)
>
> JOHN: Who? Oh, of course.

86

DIANA: She says you're a senior at Riverdale. I think that's wonderful.

WINIFRED: (*uncomfortable*) Wouldn't anyone like a Coca-Cola or anything? John? Diana?

JOHN: (*gazing at* DIANA) A ginger ale would be terrific.

DIANA: Two ginger ales, Winnie.

(*Blackout.*)

The doorbell is ringing. This is it! My hands flutter up to my hair, then down to smooth imaginary wrinkles from the skirt of my blue shirtwaist. Crossing the living room I am praying fervently, please make her do what I asked, God, even though it's crazy!

John is wearing his friendly grin and a letter sweater. "Hi," he says, "How're you?"

Seeing him, my confidence explodes. "I'm great," I say. "How're you?"

"You look great," he tells me.

I blush. "So do you," I reply. "Would you like something to drink?"

"Are your parents here?"

"No."

"I'll have a beer then. Is that okay?"

"Oh, *sure*, I'll get it."

"Hi."

It's Diana. I'll kill her, I swear it. "Diana, this is John. John, Diana."

They greet each other.

Wonder: they do not fall into each other's arms.

Instead, Diana follows me into the kitchen, whispering, "He's adorable!"

"Shhh," I say. "Do you really think so?"

"He's perfect for you."

"Not so loud!" I whisper, "Really?"

She is right though. He is perfect for me. The right height, weight, sense of humor—a perfect fit. As I hand him his beer, I think he is beautiful without actually being handsome. That's what is so special about him. He glows.

"What should we do, go to a movie?"

"I don't know," I say.

"Do you have a paper?"

I get the *Times.*

"Okay, let's see . . . *Baby Doll* is supposed to be terrible; Fellini's *La Strada*; *Lust for Life* with Kirk Douglas—not a chance—and *The Third Man,* which I've seen."

"Didn't you love it?"

"*Citizen Kane* was better."

"I never saw that."

"Oh, God, I keep forgetting she's only thirteen," he remarks to the ceiling.

"I can't wait to see it. I love Orson Welles."

He sighs. We look at each other's mouths for a moment, and I want to kiss him so much it makes me have to clear my throat and swallow. He offers me his beer, smiling.

"We don't have to go to the movies," he says. "Why don't we take a walk and maybe then go hear some music someplace. You want to?"

In the park I am flying. Nothing we say makes any sense and it is all hilariously funny. I think that if

88

he didn't have hold of my hand I would definitely leave the earth—I am that light.

"I know a great little place on 79th Street where we can hear some music if you'd like."

"Sure." Without a doubt I would go to the moon with him if he asked, so why not 79th Street? "What kind of music?"

"Any kind you like."

"Any kind I like? What kind of place is it, anyway?"

"My place."

"My parents are extremely well-trained," he explains, closing the door and turning on a small lamp. "They leave me alone on the weekends." Going to the record player with his coat still on, he says, "I want to play you something fantastic I bet you haven't heard. Do you like classical music?"

"Yes."

"Bach, Vivaldi, Brahms?"

I nod enthusiastically.

"Well, this is different. It's by Bartók."

"Never heard of him."

"Just wait. It's called *Concerto for Orchestra.* Listen."

With our coats on, we sit on the edge of the bed, listening. At first I'm not sure the phonograph is working, and I'm about to ask him about it when I pick up the faintest first swell of the orchestra. Then, as the music builds, I feel that I am being transported entirely away: from words, from the room, from my body.

"Take off your coat now, okay?" he whispers at the end of the record, helping me do it. "Would you like to hear the other side?"

I would like to kiss you, I think, nodding.

He turns the record over and removes his coat. Then he returns to the bed and lies down.

Now what do I do? If I lie down too, he might think I want to make out with him, and what if he doesn't want to?

Maybe he's only interested in listening to Bartók.

Meanwhile, the music has taken off without me. I'm stranded on the edge of the bed. But not for long.

"Hey," John calls from the shadows where he's propped up on an elbow.

"Hi," I say foolishly.

"I want to tell you something."

"Okay."

"Could you come over here?"

I could and do. I face him on my elbow with my legs half hanging over the edge somewhere behind me.

"I think you're pretty."

His words cover me with confusion. I turn my head away, fearing that if he takes another look he'll change his mind. But he reaches for me with his hand, turns my face around and leaves his hand on my neck. Bartók, at the same moment, becomes so lyrical it makes me want to faint.

"Don't be afraid of me," he says, "I promise I won't hurt you." He makes me feel like some small, delicate creature—a little doe maybe, or a bird.

"I'm your friend no matter what," he says. "You can trust me."

"I do trust you," I assure him. "I think you're very sane."

"That's because I told you you were pretty." He grins.

"No." I am embarrassed again. "*That* was crazy."

"You're pretty sane too, for a head-shrinker's daughter. Most head-shrinkers' children are crazy."

"Who says?"

"Everyone. But I think you're pretty well-adjusted."

I don't like the idea of being well-adjusted.

"Well," I say, "don't be too sure."

10

DIANA AND I ARE washing the picture window in our beach house. It was installed last summer for a better view of Long Island Sound. Watching her dreamily wiping clean the glass, I think she looks just like a movie star. But when I go outside to tell her, she says, "Don't be an ass!" Then, after a little reflection, she wonders. "Do you really think so?"

Visible behind her, a dead low tide; mussel beds where the marsh grasses grow. We are in Connecticut for a June weekend and it is warm. What is more, John is coming up this evening on the train. I tell Diana that half the time I'm positive I'm out of my mind.

"That's because I tortured you when you were

little." She sighs. "I used to tell you you were ugly and things like that, even before you could talk. I fed you prunes with the pits in them when no one was looking."

"Diana!"

"It's true. You were so cute and cheerful and everyone thought you were so adorable and *nice*. It made me furious, because I'd been the little queen till you came along. And then, of course, Daddy went overseas."

Since I was only six months old at the time, my memory of his departure for World War II is second-hand. Still, I can see it: Grand Central Station. My mother carrying me in her arms, Diana clutching my father's uniform and sobbing—begging him to *please* take her along.

"I was just entering the Oedipal phase," she tells me, "so it was very traumatic. You couldn't have picked a worse time to be born."

"So I'm responsible for your problems?"

"Some of them. And I'm responsible for some of yours."

"I'll forgive you if you'll forgive me."

"Well, it isn't that simple. That's why there are psychiatrists. There are things you can't forgive because you can't even *remember* them."

"Maybe they're better off forgotten."

"Father says you need to remember them in order to understand yourself."

"I'd like to understand myself," I say.

"Wouldn't we all?" my father says, strolling up with his tennis racket on his shoulder and sweat dripping from his face.

"Father," I say, "is it true what everybody says about head-shrinkers' children being crazier than everybody else?"

"What a thing to think!" my mother says, walking onto the porch, also carrying her tennis racket but sweating less.

My father says, "Well, I think it's a hard thing for people to be objective about—it's a loaded question."

"It's true," I say. "Everyone's prejudiced against us."

"That's nonsense," says my mother.

"What she means is that people have an emotional bias. After all, the name 'head-shrinker' isn't exactly neutral, is it?"

"It's disgusting," Diana says.

"I think it's very interesting," he says, "if you put aside your emotional bias and see it objectively. It tells you something about people's unconscious fears. They're very primitive. What people are really afraid of is the most primitive parts of themselves."

"Now, that's brilliant, Father," I say. "Don't you think that's *brilliant*, Mother?"

"Yes, dear," my mother says, her eyes closed in the bright sun.

"Having your head shrunk involves getting in touch with the oldest, most hidden, and, therefore, scariest parts of your mind," he explains.

"And you think everyone should face their fears, right?" I ask.

"Some of them. I don't recommend that people get into lions' cages simply because they happen to be afraid of lions."

"But if you got rid of all your fears, you could get into lions' cages and not get hurt, right?"

My mother sighs. "I just hope you aren't planning to try it," she says.

It is after midnight. I have been waiting for my sister to fall asleep. I thought she was sleeping about half an hour ago, and I started to get up and tiptoe out, but she turned over and said, "Where are you going?" so I had to say, "To the bathroom."

Every single floor board along the entire, endless hallway creaks. I inch forward, feeling my way along the wall. Passing my parents' bedroom, which is right across the hall from the guest room, I can hear my mother clear her throat. She sounds terribly awake. What would she do if she knew that I was four feet away from her, creeping down the chilly hall in my nightgown toward John in his bed? Would she try and stop me? Make a loud fuss in the middle of the night? It is doubtful.

John is waiting in his pajamas at the door of the guest room. He draws me inside and closes the door silently. It is so exciting.

"What took you so long?" he whispers, leading me over to the bed.

"Diana had insomnia," I say. "I don't think my mother is asleep yet either. God!" I am shivering.

"It's all right. Sit down. Hey, your feet are like ice cubes."

"I'm sorry."

"Don't be sorry."

"I'm not.

"I thought you might not come."

"I said I would."

"You might have fallen asleep."

"But I'm wide awake."

"Me too." We are lying on the bed. I have my arms around him, and he stroking my back. "Listen," he says, "I have to tell you something."

"Something bad?"

"Well, no."

"Something good, then."

"As a matter of fact, it isn't exactly good, either. I got the job in Maine. I leave the first of July."

"Oh, that's not bad."

"It isn't?"

"No, it's terrible! But I don't want to think about it. I refuse to believe July will ever come."

"I'll come back."

"No, you won't," I say, holding him tighter. "You're going to college in Worcester, Massachusetts, next fall and I'll never see you after that. But if I pay attention to every minute, the time won't pass and you'll never leave."

We are silent. Touching him, I forget where we are and how we got here. The whole world becomes no bigger than the space our bodies occupy, and time's not allowed to intrude. I love his skin. I have learned from him the art of kissing so that our mouths merge. It is delicious, like sinking into silk or fur. It makes me think of Mowgli, the wolf boy lying on top of the black panther. This is how good I always imagined Mowgli must feel.

John clears his throat. "What about taking off your nightgown?" he says.

"What?"

"Your nightgown," he says, sort of tugging at it. "Wouldn't you like to take it off?"

"I don't know. I'm embarrassed."

"Don't be. I'll take off my pajamas. That way you'll be able to see all of me and I'll be able to see all of you. Won't that be nice?"

"God, John, what if somebody comes in?"

He hesitates for a moment. "Nobody's coming in," he says reassuringly.

"How do you know? The house could burn down. There could be a robbery. What if the police came? What are you doing?"

"Helping you off with your nightgown."

"Oh."

"There. Want to unbutton my pajamas?"

"Oh, God."

"It's easy, see?"

"You aren't really going to . . . listen, this could be very traumatic. I want you to know that before you go any further."

He stops. Then he clears his throat again. After a little while he says, "Under my pajamas I have exactly the same anatomical arrangement as every other male human being on earth. And believe me, I've lived with it all my life: there's nothing to be afraid of."

But, I am thinking, what if I think it's horrible, then what will I do?

"Fear is all in the imagination," he tells me. "It's not real. I'm real."

Gradually, he unbuttons his pajama top and takes it off. I feel almost dreamy, but everything is vividly clear.

"You see? Reality isn't so bad," he says, slipping out of his pajama bottoms, "is it?"

"No, it's . . ."

"What?"

"Sort of a little funny."

"Terrific! Well, at least you haven't fainted from the shock."

"Oh, no, I didn't mean . . ."

"That's okay. It *is* a little comical."

"No, I think you're beautiful, really."

"So are you."

"Thank you. Now what do we do?"

11

For lack of sleep, John and I resemble two corpses
who have washed up on the beach. Luckily, it is
warm enough to lie in the sun, so no one is suspicious. Half dozing, I feel my mind swelling and
rising, like some gaseous substance, in the heat.

Time is not real. Even though the day has come,
I am still living in the experience of last night. It is
still going on. It can go on forever, in a way. I let
myself go back into it. I feel the length of John's
smooth bare body next to mine. I am still inside that
dreaminess, as though we are floating aimlessly in
space.

When we were naked, he said that I could trust
him, he wouldn't go too far. I thought that was

funny. There was no question of not trusting him. There was no question of going too far. Wherever we went would be perfect. But he didn't want to run the risk of traumatizing me, and besides, he said, it wasn't necessary.

I wanted to know if he'd ever gone too far with anyone. He hadn't. Didn't he want to? Sure, but he wasn't in a hurry. Oh, I said, I thought boys were always in a hurry. To prove themselves, you know. But John always says he doesn't have to prove anything, and I believe him.

When I turn my head to look, his face is totally relaxed in the sunlight, like a child's.

My parents love him. Over lunch he talks to my father about becoming a psychoanalyst. He would like to be a lay analyst, which means he wouldn't have to go to medical school. But my father says it would be hard to get trained unless he went to England. I am not in favor of John's going to England. Maine is bad enough.

Mother thinks it's wonderful that he's spending the summer in Maine—she always loved it as a girl, even though the water was too cold for swimming. She asks him where the camp is that he'll be working at. "Just outside of Portland," he replies.

"Is it a coed camp?" she wants to know.

"Yes." He glances at me quickly and then looks down at the sand. "There are about a hundred and fifty kids in all. I went there myself when I was twelve, so I know pretty much what to expect."

"That's nice. Do they have some sort of C.I.T.

program? You know, Winifred hasn't got anything to do this summer, maybe you could—"

"MOTHER!" I interrupt, outraged.

"What?"

"Just drop it please, okay?"

"Well, you don't, you know, and you're going to be bored to death. Tell her she's going to die of boredom hanging around Westport all summer. What she should do is get a job even if it didn't pay, or she could go to school somewhere."

"I swear to God, Mother . . . Could we talk about this later, please?"

"That's it," she says, "I'm not going to say another word. John, you talk to her, darling, won't you?"

In the city, we meet in Central Park every afternoon during the week and neck passionately on secluded benches for an hour or two. At night we talk on the phone. He has a phone of his own next to his bed, and I can call him on it any time I want, the later the better since we are both studying for finals.

Or trying to. What I am doing, really, is waiting for the weekends when we will once more be able to lie together and drift timelessly, thoughtlessly in space. I admit it: it's what I live for.

But July is approaching terrifyingly fast.

I have resigned myself to being bored in Westport. A week before he has to leave, John and I are leaning over the railing of a bridge that arches across the bridle path in Central Park. An elderly lady glides by beneath us on her privately owned horse, a chestnut mare whose neck curves like a swan's.

"When I was little, I wanted to be a horse like that," I say, "but everyone told me I couldn't."

"Well," he shrugs, "you can't."

"No, but I knew how much easier it would have been. This is so difficult—your going away. I'm sorry if it makes you feel bad to hear me say it, but I wish you didn't have to."

"It doesn't make me feel bad. It makes me feel great. But listen, I want to talk to you about that. I think we ought to maybe make some kind of agreement so that we know, you know, where we stand."

"Like what kind of agreement?" I ask apprehensively.

"I want you to know that you are perfectly free to go out with people, I mean, boys, if they appeal to you."

But who, I wonder, could appeal to me? "You do?" I say.

"And you know why? Because I love you."

"Excuse me," I say, moving unexpectedly onto the verge of tears, "but how does that work?"

"I want you to feel free to do what you want. And I don't believe in making promises."

His statement severs something inside me. I get momentarily dizzy; there is a distinct darkening of the light. I seem to have been hiking through a meadow and now I've come to the end, and on one side there is a steep gorge, and on another a dark wood, and on the other a rocky slope. And I'm alone; there are no maps, and you're not allowed to turn around.

It is terrifying.

And infuriating. John, I can tell, is perfectly at

ease, while I'm feeling so crazy it is difficult to speak.

But I'm compelled to say the right thing, even though my heart isn't in it, even though it's a lie: "Okay," I tell him, the corners of my mouth twitching tragi-comically, "I agree."

We are in John's room; it is late at night and dark—I cannot see the time. The air is heavy with heat and humidity and a slightly dank smell from the Hudson River.

The bed is a chaotic sea of twisted sheets and clothing wrinkled beyond recognition. We are in our underwear and John, who is rocking gently back and forth, reminds me of a dolphin in the waves.

In the beginning, everything seemed simpler than it does now. This is because I was naive, according to John. I didn't even know about masturbating, for example, which is something boys do frequently, he told me. Boys are different. Fascinating. If a boy gets really excited, it's supposed to be painful for him not to have an orgasm. No one ever told me that before. Nevertheless, I now believe it is a Fact of Life.

What amazes me is that boys aren't more embarrassed about the whole thing. I would be. I sort of am, I guess.

But boys aren't the same. Right now, for example, I have no *idea* what John is feeling or what it feels like to be John. This might be because *he* doesn't seem to be aware of *me* at all. He doesn't realize I'm uncomfortable, that I can't breathe too well, or that my left leg's falling asleep. I wouldn't want to interrupt and tell him so, either. One thing I have decided is: I don't ever want to make John suffer. Even if I have to suffer instead.

His breath is deafening, his T-shirt wringing wet. I am aware that our real selves are drifting apart, even though our bodies press closer together.

It's all happening so fast, so violently. What would it be like, then, to go all the way, I wonder, if simply touching someone is so dangerous?

Deep down, I have a feeling it could kill you or possibly drive you crazy.

John sighs and stops moving.

The next day he is gone.

12

IN JULY MY FATHER comes to Westport only on the weekends. Mother plays tennis every morning at eight o'clock, gardens madly, and repaints the guest room for the third time. Diana goes to Silvermine Art School and paints three mornings a week. Afternoons, she gazes wistfully across the Sound at Long Island where Randy Robbin is working as a caddy.

When the tide is right, I fish.

My father buys the bait for me in town: hideous sea worms with wriggling legs and mean pincers in their heads. Disgusting.

When the tide is not right for fishing, I walk over the sand flats to the town beach. Sometimes I see people I know. Chris, for example, who looks like a handsome monkey and gives me surreptitious puffs of his Marlboros, Winstons, and Pall Malls; or Micky, who was kicked out of school last year for stealing cars. They're both sixteen. At night they cruise the diner, stop for a Dairy Queen, and maybe drive through the yacht club before ending up on one of the bridges near my house to drink beer. Sometimes Micky lets me drive his car, which is really his mother's. It's a hydramatic. He maintains a chimpanzee could drive it with a blindfold on, but I find it thrilling.

Today I see them, along with Marge, a girl who has fingernails like the Witch of the North in *The Wizard of Oz*. Also Patty, who is fat because her father owns a delicatessen. Sitting down on the sand, I decide, we are a pretty motley crew, all in all.

Everyone stares into space for a while. Nothing is happening after all. Since the tide began to go out, the wind has died. There hasn't been a cloud in the sky for days. It is hot, even for July. Chris, who has red hair, is pink beneath his freckles.

"You want to try a Kool?" he asks me, proffering a pack.

I dart a look over my shoulder (you never know who might be watching) and take one.

"These are gross, if you ask me," Micky says, also taking one but lighting it separately because three on a match means bad luck.

After four puffs of my Kool, I'm practically too dizzy to sit up. Along with the nausea, I feel guilt. This is terrible—thirteen-year-old girls shouldn't smoke cigarettes. But they shouldn't be bored to death, either! And there is *absolutely nothing inter-esting to do*! And what is more, it's too hot to think. I want to make something happen! What? Excite-ment. Romance. Music and dancing even, now we're talking! I want *action*.

We are going to the movies. My sister, my father, his wife, and me. We—that is me and my mother—aren't speaking to each other. She doesn't like my attitude or something. I have no idea, *believe* me, why. My father doesn't want to get involved. "Leave me out of it," is all he asks.

We have been waiting on line for an eternity, and Diana and I are getting on each other's nerves. At last the theater doors swing open, and the audience from the early show begins filing out. My father comes out of his reverie and smiles at us. When Diana edges in front of me, I cannot resist pinching her. She responds by stepping on my toe. Now my toe feels broken and I can't even complain because I started it. Shit. I'm going to sit next to Father. My mother and my sister can both go to hell.

I turn around. My father is casually watching the exit line when I see something strange flash across his expression, and turning toward the wall, he coughs self-consciously. A second later, our line be-gins to move, and he inches deliberately forward, his head bent and turned to the side.

I wonder: who is he trying to avoid? And why? I can't imagine. Then, as we are getting our tickets torn, it occurs to me that this riddle has a simple answer, which some trick of my mind prevents me from getting. Because, I inwardly sigh, I'm an idiot.

Streaks of vermillion dawn across the flat mirror of water. For a moment, everything appears as one still point. Then a sudden sense of expectancy stirs inside me, and I hear a gull cry.

Getting into my bathing suit, I go downstairs and walk along the beach. In the sunrise, my skin is a deep cocoa against the sand, except of course where my bathing suit is. There it is porcelain, but no one knows. I can't believe the colors: an agate sky; emerald grasses; the water like an opal with its sun-fire. And it is *hot*, even though the sun isn't fully up yet. The sand is cool.

The coast, as far as I can see, is empty. I feel as though I am the only one awake in the world. Suppose it were true, like in some science-fiction story? Everyone except me might be under the power of a drug or something from outer space and remain sleeping forever. I could have anything I wanted. It would be lonely, though. Maybe there'd be someone else . . . Marlon Brando! He would take me in his arms and we would ride horses through the jungle. . . . God!

A sudden human sound causes my whole body to snap into automatic rigidity. I am poised for flight.

There is a person—male—cradled in the rock to my right. The only other thing I know is that I've entirely lost contact with the ground.

Again, he makes the sound that first riveted my attention—a discreet cough. "Hello," he says.

I meet his eyes.

"Not a bad sunrise," he says.

His eyes are very serious in the center. I nod.

"It was so hot I couldn't sleep, so I drove out here to the state park. Do you live over there?" He gestures toward the cove, which is half-visible around a bend in the coast.

"Yes," I tell him, still quaking.

"Those are just summer houses, right?"

He is partially shaded by the rock, but the sun, coming up to my right in a glaring swirl of fire, is melting the shadows. His voice is natural and reassuring. My knees experience a sudden release of tension. It's okay: I can put the thought of running out of my mind. I take a few deep breaths. "Yes," I reply (that's better), "they're just summer houses."

"I'm spending the weekend up near Black Rock Turnpike. Do you know where that is?"

His hair is quite long. One dark shock of it is lifted by the breeze and swept rakishly across his forehead to conceal one eye.

"I've been there. To Robert Penn Warren's house," I say, feeling suddenly expansive. "Do you know Robert Penn Warren?"

"No."

"Neither do I. But there were a bunch of his books around, and I didn't like any of them."

"Oh," he says, tilting his head slightly and gazing impishly from underneath his hair, "neither do I."

"I'm really glad to hear you say that," I confide. "I always doubt my own judgment. It's very neurotic of me, my father says. He's a psychoanalyst."

"Is he?" he says, leaning forward. Then he stands

abruptly up into the sunlight. He looks about eighteen. He isn't very tall, I notice. His narrow, attractive, and very sunburned face almost looks familiar.

"Have I seen you somewhere?" I wonder.

"The other night at the movie," he says. "Remember?"

The movie . . . Tony Curtis (whose real name is Bernard Schwartz) married Janet Leigh (his real wife). That's all I remember about the movie. "Oh, sure," I say, not wanting to hurt his feelings.

"It wasn't very good."

"No."

"I was thinking of maybe taking a swim."

"It's hot enough," I tell him.

"Want to join me?"

Walking by his side toward the water, I'm certain I don't remember seeing him at the movie. . . . What if he's a psychopathic killer? And nobody around . . . Winifred, you must be crazy after all. On the other hand, I reconsider, what if he's not? He seems . . . what? Interesting and smart. But strange—it's in his eyes.

We float on the marble-smooth surface of Long Island Sound. With his straight hair parted and drops of water clinging to the thick lashes of his eyes, he reminds me of a seal: sleek, swift, and unpredictable.

"Do you like being the daughter of a psychoanalyst?"

"Sure, but I've never been anything else."

"But you can imagine."

"Yes, but it's not the same. Anyway, sometimes I'm not even sure if anyone else really exists. I know it's crazy," I say, and stop, suddenly embarrassed to have given so much away.

"It isn't crazy, go ahead."

"When I was a little girl, I used to have the feeling that people were only real when I was there with them. The minute I stopped perceiving them—poof! They disappeared. Not that they died, but they went into another dimension. I can't really explain it."

"I know what you mean."

"You do?"

"Exactly. I used to experience the exact same thing."

"Hey, do you ever get derealized? Here's what it feels like: you're at a party, say, and everyone is talking and all of a sudden it's almost like you're in a tunnel: your vision sort of telescopes and everything gets *totally* unreal. My father calls it derealization."

He tries to picture it and says, "I think I know what you mean."

How nice, I think. I like him.

We swim for a while, out into the tranquil Sound, then turn and face the shore, treading water.

"Are you in college?" I ask.

"Uh-huh."

"Which college?"

He pauses, just for a moment, then says, "N.Y.U."

"Oh. Do you want to race in?"

He gives me a headstart and wins anyway.

"You're fast," I pant. "Wow!"

"Yeah," he says breathlessly, "but I have no endurance."

He has a red Thunderbird convertible! On the seat is a towel and a pack of Winstons.

He offers me the towel.

"Oh, that's okay," I tell him.

"Go ahead, dry your hair with it."

"Is this your car? It's terrific."

"Well, it runs all right, but I think it's a little flashy, really. It belongs to my sister, who's living with some guy in Rome."

Wow, I think, how *interesting*! "How old is she?"

"Nineteen. We're twins."

"Really?"

"Her name is ... Isabel. What's yours?"

"Winifred."

"Of course," he tells me, "how perfect."

I do not know what is so perfect about it, but I agree to meet him tomorrow: same time, same place. His name is Timothy Wilding III. I walk home along the beach feeling a little seasick, probably from being hungry.

13

"OUR PARENTS HAVE been dead for years," Timothy explains, fishing a pack of Winstons out of his glove compartment. "We were brought up by an aunt and uncle, a very rich aunt and uncle, in Boston. I came to New York at fifteen to go to college. Right now I'm working on my M.A."

"That's fantastic."

"It's actually a crashing bore," he says, leading me toward the beach and shifting his hair out of his eyes with a quick toss of his head. "What I want to be is a playwright."

This is getting better all the time. "A playwright?"

"It's in my blood," he sighs. "Both my parents were on the stage. My mother was sixteen when she ran off with my father, a Shakespearean actor from England. He was almost forty at the time. Her family disinherited her, of course, but when she died of TB at twenty-six, Isabel and I went to live in her family's mansion on Beacon Hill. My father returned to London, but didn't last the year. His heart gave out, or something."

"How awful."

"Yes."

This is amazing, I think. What a fascinating person! "Your life is like a novel," I say.

"Not a very good one," he says, bowing his head so his hair obscures his eyes again.

"Oh, you just think that because it's yours. I think it's great."

He looks up, suddenly radiant. "Do you really?"

"Yes."

Grinning, he bows low and flourishes an imaginary cape, asking, "Would you like a cigarette? You *are* old enough to smoke, aren't you?"

It isn't right to lie, I know, but I'm so flattered, I say, "Sure I am. Thanks," and take one.

Winstons aren't as strong as Kools, but it is only 6 A.M. and I haven't had anything to eat, so I try not to inhale too much of the smoke. The excess gets into my nose anyway, and within moments I feel ill.

"Tell me more about yourself," Timothy is saying.

"Me? Like what?"

"Well, do you have any brothers or sisters, for example?"

"I have a sister." Given my queasiness, talking is a struggle. "She's three years older than me, almost, and her name is Diana and she's beautiful." I always have to get that out in the beginning, I notice.

"More beautiful than you?"

"Oh, *yes*. Much."

"She must be fantastic."

I wish I didn't feel like vomiting. I might enjoy this.

"What's she like? Are you friends?"

"Sometimes. We fight a lot."

"She probably tries to tyrannize you."

"She does."

"Humiliate you."

"*Yes.*"

"She's jealous of you, obviously."

"Of me?"

"Naturally."

"It's because I'm easier to get along with," I admit. "Diana's very suspicious. She'd never have spoken to you. Once we were on a train coming home from Pennsylvania by ourselves. We went to the dining car and each got a glass of milk. We must have been very cute. When we went to pay the check, the waiter said it had been taken care of by the two gentlemen in the corner. Well, I thought it was a great idea, but my sister became utterly outraged. She stormed over to their table, slammed down her fifty-cent piece, and marched out of the dining car. She was only seven then, but she hasn't changed a bit."

Having talked my way out of the nausea, I am pleasantly relaxed and feel like talking more.

"She doesn't let anyone get too close," I muse. "Once she told me it was because everyone always told her how beautiful she was. It made her feel they only saw the outside of her, and that made her feel empty on the inside. Of course, she isn't at all empty, she's rather amazing really, but sometimes she hides so well even she can't find herself. Sometimes she's invisible. I, on the other hand, have the opposite problem."

"What's that?"

"Sometimes I let people see too much."

I don't tell anyone about my secret meetings on the beach at sunrise because they leave me feeling slightly squeamish, don't ask me why. I consider mentioning Timothy in a letter I am writing to John, but I decide he might get the wrong impression. Besides it would be premature. What is more, I bet John is doing the same thing in Maine, not that I'm *doing* anything, of course, which he probably is.

Our first evening meeting is on a jetty in mid-August. Strong smells rise off the barnacle-covered pilings and the sand flats, which have been baking in the sun. The tide is coming in at the end of the jetty; some fishermen are catching eels in the shallows.

As usual, Timothy makes me feel like talking. I say, "Last summer I went fishing with my parents and we ran into a school of eels. I thought my mother would lose her mind entirely. She got hysterical. My father thought it was a riot. The eels kept wriggling out of his hands and slithering all around the boat. It was *disgusting*. But he insisted on cooking two of them for dinner. He even made a secret pact with me to say they tasted good, no matter what. My mother wouldn't go near my father all night. She said it was because he ate the eels, but really it was because he'd been mean to her."

"My uncle—the rich one who brought me up—he was cruel. He knew how to make people feel weak. Then he could have power over them. Perhaps he was a bit like your father. Doctors have more power over people than anyone."

"Doctors? Don't be silly."

"And psychoanalysts most of all. Psychoanalysts don't even tell people what the hell's the matter with them!" He says it almost viciously, and I feel personally attacked.

"That's not *true*," I tell him.

"Of *course*, it's true, are you *kidding*?"

Suddenly I could strangle him. When he gets snotty and superior, I hate him. Why I even bother hanging around him is a mystery to me. I once read an Edgar Allan Poe story where a man is made to do self-destructive things by the "imp of the perverse" who lives inside him. Poe says we've all got little imps inside who try to get power over us. They have only our worst interests at heart. I imagine mine with bristly fur and sharp, pointed teeth.

Timothy grins down at me. In the reddish glow of the setting sun, his face looks ghoulish. I shiver. Without looking at me, he puts his arm around my shoulder. My flesh goes goose-pimply. "What's the matter?" he says.

"Oh, I'm just a little cold."

"I've got a blanket in the car, come on."

The truth is, I don't want to; I would rather be cold. But I don't know how to say so. Sometimes I feel as though a magic spell has been cast on me making it impossible to say no. My imp must be behind it. (He's also got nasty little bloodshot eyes, I decide.)

Timothy spreads the blanket over our bare knees in the front seat of the Thunderbird. It is coarse, army-green, and on one corner there's a name-tag that says "Mark Silverstein." A thought crosses my mind: perhaps when Timothy was a little boy he stole this army blanket off Mark Silverstein's bunk at camp, and Mark Silverstein has been freezing ever since.

Timothy turns on the radio. There is an ad for acne medicine, which I don't happen to need, thank God, followed by a stupid phone conversation with some dumb girl who wants to dedicate "You're a Thousand Miles Away" to Charlie. Even though I detest the song, it makes me think of John. I haven't heard from him in over two weeks. I'm sure he has another girl friend, prettier than me and doubtless old enough to go all the way with.

I wish I'd never even heard of sex. I wish I could get the pictures of it out of my mind: John kissing my neck, my shoulders, and other places too embarrassing to contemplate. Timothy is looking at me, but his hand is on my thigh underneath the blanket. He's touching the inside of it in some way that makes me feel so tingly and weird I want to leap out of my seat.

Thank goodness, he never comes to the house or calls me on the phone. My parents wouldn't like him, that I'm sure of. And Diana would think he was a psychopath, I know it. His hand is clammy. It makes me thing of those eels I ate, which makes me feel—quite suddenly—like throwing up.

But then I think: I'm *horrible*. He's not doing anything bad. I'm just angry because he isn't John. *Damn* John, anyway! Who does he think he is?

"Are you upset about something?" Timothy asks.

"Not at all," I reply.

"It must be me then. Nothing has been going right for some time. I feel like Hamlet; that the world is stale, flat, and unprofitable; that nothing works out the way it should; that life is too tedious, too absurd . . ."

"Timothy, that's terrible." I feel so guilty I could cry.

"Is it? It feels more or less normal to me." He sighs, leaning back and closing his eyes.

He's tragic, I tell myself, and I've been completely horrible to him. Beneath the blanket I lift his clammy hand from between my thighs and hold it.

After a minute he puts it back again and sighs again. On the radio, Fats Domino has found his thrill on Blueberry Hill. The sun has set. We are steeped in shadow. Out of the corner of my eye I see something move under the blanket in the area of Timothy's lap. A chill of revulsion crackles up my spine, and all in a flash I remember an episode that occurred when I was seven.

I was leaving my piano lesson on West 76th Street around dusk. Across the street and halfway up the block, there was a man, and the minute I saw him I knew he was all wrong. No one else was around.

119

I didn't want to seem afraid, so I crossed the street and proceeded up the block with my eyes glued to the pavement. But just as I was passing him, something compelled me to look up. I nearly fainted when I saw it, it was so enormous. I thought, "That is his penis and he is showing it to *me*."

Altogether, I've seen five exhibitionists. The others, however, were all in the park, during the day, and at a distance. My father says they aren't dangerous, but even just thinking about them now makes me feel a little faint.

Timothy's fingers have already wriggled the whole way up my thigh and are now worming their way under the cuffs of my shorts. I take a big breath, turn sideways, and cross my legs all in one frenzied motion. Timothy throws his head back and chuckles quietly for a moment. Then he pinches me hard on the ass.

"Ow!" I say. "Rat!"

"There are worse things to be," he says disgustedly, "and their initials are C.T., which stands for cock teaser, in case you didn't know."

I am astonished, outraged, furious. "That's *bull* and you know it."

"Say, how old are you, anyway, eleven?"

I wish I could think of something equally cutting and twice as clever to say to him, but I can't. So I open the car door and get out. He opens his door and gets out too. I start running for the jetty, but he grabs my arm and, twisting me around, says: "Hold it, honey."

I am amazed, and, what is more, *thrilled* by the pressure of his grip on my arm. In the twilight he looks like Montgomery Clift: shadowy and passionate. Looking into his eyes—the left one half-concealed as usual—I suddenly begin to derealize, as my father calls it. Everything seems to be receding into a tunnel; and a certain note, actually a chord, seems to come from everywhere all at once. I feel so totally unreal I might as well be playing in a movie.

"I'm sorry," I say, which isn't true, but seems like an appropriate line.

"No," he says, "there's nothing to be sorry for." He sighs and drops my arm. "Sometimes I just forget myself. I can't stand upsetting someone I care about." Then, flashing his most radiantly reassuring smile, he says, "Meet me on the beach tomorrow afternoon?"

The tunneling movement stops. The echoes fade abruptly. I didn't think I was going to get off quite so easily this time.

I am (almost) disappointed.

Automatically, I say, "Sure."

The next day my parents are on their way to play tennis as usual. I tell them I'm planning to go fishing.

It is a breezy, overcast morning, but I figure it'll clear up later. In between Elvis Presley and The Platters, the radio gives a weather forecast that I pay no attention to. Toward noon I load my equipment into the dingy with its brand new Johnson outboard, and when the tide has risen sufficiently for me to reach the channel, I leave the cove and head out into the deep and choppy waters of the Sound.

Since my anchor is quite light and the water rougher than I expected, I decide to drift in with the tide toward the public beach, where I hope to be overtaken by schools of ravenous, fast-fighting fish.

So: bait the hook with vile sea worms (they deserve to die) and cast into sea.

As my sinker hits bottom, before I've even reversed the reel, there is a sudden, dramatic tug. My rod bends, trembling, and the reel spins. My line races into the water. I throw the drag lever and the wild spinning stops. What is it? Reeling it in slow now. Certainly no flounder. Too savage.

Soon a murky form seems to swell out of the shadows . . . a sandshark. Hideous. That blunt snout, rubbery flesh, and God, the teeth.

Maybe I should kill it with an oar.

Don't get hysterical: he's swallowed the hook.

Leave him in the water. Cut the line with a knife.

Now watch him vanish, as though digested by the sea.

I think life is very strange, taking everything into account, including sharks—even if they are sandsharks—and death . . . and the fact that I have drifted halfway to Long Island. There are no boats around at all. What's going on here, anyway? OhmyGod, The radio! It said small craft warnings due to offshore winds. Now I remember. At the time, it might have been a broadcast from Venus . . . it had nothing to do with me. (What am I, crazy?)

It seems to take hours getting to shore against the

wind, and the whole time I'm worried about running out of gas.

Eventually, I see Timothy on the isolated end of the beach.

He waves.

I wave back.

I land.

"Thrilling day, I say, isn't it?" he says, the wind blowing in his hair.

"You are not kidding," I tell him, "you should see it out there. God! Did you know there were small-craft warnings out? I did, but I forgot. It's typical. I'm accident-prone, according to my father. He says I'm impulsive. I don't *think* about things, so I get into trouble."

Timothy is wearing a pair of dove-gray lederhosen, which are suede shorts from Switzerland made for climbing mountains in. I rarely feel violent about clothes, but I swear I would sell my sister for a pair of lederhosen like Timothy's. His burgundy T-shirt (French, you can tell by the alligator) is one-third in and two-thirds out of his leather pants, giving him a tousled, casual, and (I must admit it) *sexy* air.

I am feeling exhilarated, reckless. "I caught a sandshark," I announce.

"What's that?"

"A big fish that looks like a small shark and is one of the creepiest things you can imagine."

"Worse than an eel?" he says slyly.

"Don't be silly," I giggle.

"In the mood for a little drive?"

"If I can drive a little."

123

"Why not?"

"Really?"

He tosses me the keys. "Hop in," he says, "and drive me to distraction."

Timothy is a prince, I think, settling in behind the wheel of the Thunderbird. The top is down. Maybe I'm in love with him after all. I mean, this is so exciting I could *die*.

I turn the key in the ignition, smiling at him. The car starts, lurches violently forward, then expires.

"You're in gear," he informs me. "Do you know how to shift? The pattern's right there on the dash."

God! That was really dumb. Let's see . . . I find the clutch and practice shifting gears according to the diagram. My hands, however, are trembling. Do I really want to go through with this? I mean, people get killed . . .

"What're you waiting for? Just ease the clutch out slowly . . . I'll tell you what to do. That's it, now give it a little more gas . . . great. You're a regular pro. Except that's neutral. Try again."

I'm doing it. I'm hardly breathing, but I'm doing it. The sense of power is making me feel drunk. And the wind.

"Now just keep your eyes on the road," Timothy tells me, putting his hand on my neck. "And concentrate on driving."

"Timothy? I mean . . ." I don't want him to think I'm not *grateful*, but for Godsakes. "Do you really think that's safe?"

"I have perfect confidence in you," he says, reaching beneath the neck of my T-shirt to pat my shoulder.

I wish I could say the same.

We are proceeding smoothly along the nearly empty coastal road. Sharp and contradictory gusts of wind tangle my hair. I must look like the Medusa or at least the wild woman of Borneo, but I don't care.

About Timothy's hand, now stroking around my shoulders underneath my T-shirt, I do care: I cannot *bear* it and at the same time it would be worse if he stopped. Which is completely crazy.

The truth is that none of the feelings I have about Timothy make any sense. When I find him most dangerous is when I'm practically in love with him. Take now, for example. I mean, he's got his hand on the naked flesh of my—OhmyGod—*breast.* "Timothy!"

"You're doing great. You're a real pro."

What's *that* supposed to mean, I wonder. On top of everything else, now I'm feeling irritated. I mean, I am *not* a pro . . .

"HEY!" he calls. "Watch that mailbox!"

Panic. I swerve wide to avoid the mailbox, which I don't even see, just as the road curves sharply the other way. Timothy grabs the wheel and turns it hard, just as I hit the gas pedal instead of the brake.

For a horrible moment there is only confusion. Noise—motion—fear—no past or future, up or down, here or there.

Then the dust clears, and we find ourselves in the center of the road with the engine stalled, facing in the opposite direction.

"Good God!" I gasp, collapsing over the steering wheel.

"Not bad," he says casually. "Hurry up now and

switch seats with me. Hop into the back."

I do, trembling violently all over. He slithers around the gear shift into the driver's seat. "Okay," he says, "quick now. I don't think anybody saw us."

I tumble into the front seat and lie there like a sack of rags. He starts the engine and continues on down the road in the direction we just came from. Whistling. (Can you *believe* it?)

It's several minutes before I have enough control over my muscles to straighten up. When I do, Timothy glances at me sideways and grins his most innocently winning grin.

"We could have been killed," I say.

"You exaggerate."

"Injured then."

He takes my hand. "Wasn't it thrilling?" he says.

"Yes," I say, giggling in spite of myself.

He puts my hand high up on his thigh and holds it there.

Now what, I think. *God.*

We are approaching a turn-off to the Boston Post Road. A sign points the way to Cape Cod. Where did I hear Cape Cod mentioned today? I remember, on the radio. As the road bends north, I see thunderheads piling up on the horizon. Then I remember there's going to be a storm.

14

I DO NOT COME TO MY senses until after we've stopped for Timothy to put up the top. The sky has turned slate gray and missiles of rain are bombarding the windshield. At first it is just a feeling, an intuition. Then a sensation of sudden wooziness invades my body. Gradually my thoughts collect themselves: my parents will have left the tennis court hours ago. They will think I am out in the dingy. They will be frantic.

By the time we get back to the state park, the wind is fierce and an ominous blackness is spreading through the sky. The beach is empty. There is no one in sight. There is *nothing* in sight. "Good God, Timothy!" I gasp, "where's my boat?"

"Oh, no," he says, scanning the part of the beach —now covered by sea—where we left it insecurely moored.

"I don't believe it!" I say, madly scrambling over the top of the door in my haste to get out of the car. "My father's new Johnson, *God*!"

Timothy has already flung open his door and leapt onto the beach. Without looking back he dashes knee-deep into the surf, frantically scanning the Sound in all directions.

"This is the end," I say approaching. "My father is going to have a fit."

"Shut up!" he says, without turning around. "Just shut *up* for one minute."

"Are you nuts?"

"Goddamn it!" he says, wheeling around. "This is *serious*."

I am staring at him, dumbfounded. Both of us are drenched with the pelting rain. "What's the matter?" I say.

"I don't want to be implicated in this, okay? This is *your* fault."

"I know that," I say. "Don't be so angry," and I turn to go, confused and what is more, wounded.

"Will you meet me here tomorrow?" he asks, his tone softening.

"I can't promise," I say.

"Never mind then," he says, roughly again. "Just remember to leave me out of it."

He's positively irrational, I think. "Don't worry!" I yell over my shoulder. And then I'm off—racing down the beach toward home just as a lightning bolt slashes through the sky to light up the rain-battered, wind-swept coast. This is followed by a clap of thunder so violent it could only signify, I think, the outbreak of war.

It's as bad as it could be. Even through the rain from far away, I can see hordes of people on our beach. Across the wet sand I dash, across rocks and oblivious to broken shells, pain.

Everybody is gathered at my house, and what is more, there is a large white boat idling just offshore. It has big black letters on it: Harbor Police.

My father is not on the beach; he left an hour ago in the motorboat to try and find me. Then the police boat arrived towing the empty dingy. My mother is in a state of shock. Everyone was sure I had fallen overboard and most likely drowned. So they all listen attentively, police included, when I finally catch my breath and begin stuttering out my explanation: I was fishing when I realized there were offshore winds. I headed for home but was forced to land on the public beach. I didn't realize a storm was brewing and took a walk with a girl friend I happened to meet. The anchor was light, the tide high, and it was stupid of me, but I didn't mean to worry anyone. "I'm so sorry," I say, and start to cry.

It works. My mother hugs me, and everyone pats everyone else's soaking wet shoulders and says, "Thank God, she's all right." The rain is stopping. The storm is passing. I am saved.

But not for long.

When my father returns, after several hours of searching the Sound, he is drenched, chilled to the bone, and so upset over my "behavior" (as he keeps calling it) that I begin to wish I had drowned after all.

Two martinis, a hot shower, and dry clothes do not temper his outrage. An hour passes, dinner is served, and still he is harping on my behavior. He is starting to get on my nerves.

"What I can't understand is how you could have left it below the high-water mark with the tide coming in," he says, and not for the first time, either.

"I thought it was up high enough, I told you that," I say irritably.

"But it obviously wasn't."

"*Obviously.*"

"So obviously you weren't aware of what you were doing, isn't that right?"

"Daddy"—I sort of snarl—"leave me alone."

"Answer me."

"NO!"

Violent thoughts are erupting inside me: dynamite beneath the house is wired to explode—all I have to do is press on the left arm of this chair and . . . WHAM!!

My mother says, "*Arthur*, you're not giving her a chance."

"Look," my father says, changing his position and trying, without success, to sound reasonable, "can't you understand my concern?"

"Nothing *happened*," I whine.

"Well, that's where we disagree," he says hotly, "because I happen to think a great deal happened. You left a boat with a brand-new outboard engine

130

on it abandoned on a public beach with the tide coming in in a storm. I don't call that nothing happening, I call it impulsive behavior!"

"I *know* that," I tell him, clenching my teeth in rage. "So what?"

"So I think you have an impulse neurosis!"

"A *what?*" Now I am really ready to kill him. If this dynamite worked, he'd be in smithereens right now, I swear it.

But he goes on, his tone aggressive, his words cutting like swords: "Your tendency to forget critical details, your habit of leaping into things without looking to see what the hell they are, I think these may be problems you need some help with!"

"I THINK YOU'RE OUT OF YOUR GOD-DAMN MIND!" I scream at him, having passed the limits of my self-control.

My mother intervenes. "Enough is enough, Arthur," she says.

Even Diana, scowling, sides with us: "Really, Father, you've been harping on this for hours."

"You're just trying to have power over me!" I say, without really thinking.

Silent, he picks at the skin around his thumbnails, a habit he has. "I think I'll go lie down. I'm tired," he says.

He pulls himself up and walks wearily across the rush carpet to the stairs. The three of us sit quietly, listening to his footsteps and the creaking of the floorboards down the hall. I know it is just a rest between battles in a long campaign, but I am no less grateful for his absence.

It's a long time before anybody speaks.

Then Diana says, "Don't feel bad. It'll pass."

And my mother says, "Do try to be more careful, darling, you know it's worth it to avoid these kinds of scenes."

"It *was* rather dumb—" Diana begins.

"Don't you start on me, I swear I'll—"

"But you might think a little bit about what he said," Diana says.

"I think she's thought enough for one day," says my mother.

I respond with a wave of self-pity: Poor Me. Followed by a surge of indignation: He'll be Sorry!

I wake up with a start. I'm in a sweat. Immense relief at being out of that dream. I don't even want to think about it. What was it, anyway? I was going to the dentist, that's right. But the elevator let me off at 10, and there was a sign on his door: Office— Ring Bell and Walk In, which was odd, but I did it anyway. Then I can't remember . . . wait a minute! The dentist was examining someone's teeth. Wow! Here's the weird part: the patient was Timothy. What is more, he was tied to the chair. Powerless. And the dentist was pulling out his teeth. The dentist said that was the only way to stop the pain.

Haze today. My head feels like it's all stuffed up with foam rubber.

Since I know my father has an early tennis date, I resolve to fix him breakfast, the way I used to . . . when we were friends.

I boil water, set the table, even cut around the

sections of a grapefruit. The bagels Mother brought up from New York are hard as rocks. So I take the sharpest knife from the rack and, holding a bagel in my left hand, start to sever it lengthwise. No sooner do I apply pressure, than the blade skids sideways and whizzes downward, opening a huge gash in the mound of soft flesh at the base of my thumb.

I go rigid. From beneath the bagel a river of blood is spurting rhythmically over my arm, the counter, and finally, as I stand there frozen with amazement, the floor. I lunge for the sink—showering blood on my shirt and my neatly carved grapefruit. I turn on the cold water, thrust in my hand, and observe the damage. It is worse than I'd imagined: at the bottom of the wound lies a satiny white glimmer of bone.

It certainly ranks as a major accident, I think. Maybe I'll faint . . . no, I guess not. Eventually, my hand grows numb. I bind it in a clean dish towel and raise it above my head. With my knees trembling violently, I am trying to clean up some of the mess when my father comes through the door. He is dressed for tennis, immaculate in his whites. As though a switch has been thrown, I burst into tears.

"Oh my God." He says it quietly, like a statement. "What were you doing?"

"Cutting a bagel."

"I can't stand it."

"I'm sorry, Father, really . . ."

He heaves a long, resigned sigh, a sigh so sad he might be looking across a battlefield of dying soldiers. "Let me see . . ." he says.

"It's horrible," I tell him, not moving.

Again the sigh. "Come on, pussy . . . Oh, my God!"

"I told you."

"I can't stand it." He is grimacing in pain.

"Neither can I."

"Can you move your thumb?"

"I don't know, it hurts."

"I can't stand it."

"Daddy, you keep *saying* that."

"I can't help it."

"It hurts you more than it hurts me."

"I know."

"I'll need stitches, won't I?"

"At least."

"What else?"

"That depends upon the tendon. Goodness, Winifred, how do you manage these things?"

Panic. "What tendon?"

Sigh. "The one that moves your thumb around. Now hold still, pussy-cat, and let me wrap your hand again."

"There is no point in being irrational," my father tells my mother. "She's going to be fine."

"Well, why aren't you *doing* something? Why don't you call in somebody *local* since you can't get Greenspan in New York?"

"I *am* getting Greenspan in New York; his service is calling him now."

"Oh, he could be *anywhere*. This child is bleeding to death!"

Although we did have to change the dish towel, her statement is exaggerated. I am calm now, resigned. I feel only distantly related to the present circumstances; it is already just another action-packed episode of my life.

My father is saying, "Listen, if she severed a tendon, we're going to need a hand surgeon."

"Oh, my God! Winifred, how could you *do* such a thing?!"

Diana, supporting my arm in the air, says, "Stop screaming, Mother."

My mother stops, takes a deep breath, and sobs. "My darling—"

The phone rings.

"Hello, Gerry? Arthur. Sorry to trouble you. No, I'm all right; it's Winnie. She's opened up her *flexor pollicis longus* with a knife. . . . I can't tell. . . . We could meet you there in an hour. Sorry. Thanks."

We are driving down the West Side Highway, which shimmers in the heat. My father clears his throat. "I've been thinking," he says. "Something more is going on here than meets the eye."

"Like what?"

"Well, I think you may be troubled about something you aren't even aware of: you may be repressing something you feel guilty about. Repressed guilt often comes out in neurotic or self-destructive ways."

I feel a twinge of acute discomfort. Whatever happens, I think, I refuse to be neurotic.

"Everyone has guilt, you know. It's part of the human condition."

"Are we born with it?"

"No." He sighs. "It has to be learned. You probably learn it from your parents."

"Gee," I say, "thanks a bunch."

In the emergency room of Mt. Sinai Hospital several babies are expressing loud disapproval of the human condition. We enter a white-curtained cubicle where Dr. Greenspan is waiting with a nurse. She carefully unwraps my hand. He wants to know how I managed it.

"Cutting a bagel," I reply.

"From now on only English muffins," he tells me. "You can open them with a fork."

He promises I won't feel a thing. My father helps me lie down on the examining table. Suddenly, I feel completely helpless and afraid. But I'm determined not to show it. Out of the corner of my eye, I see the nurse stick a hypodermic needle into a jar. A yellow fluid flows into the syringe.

"Did you know," Dr. Greenspan says, leaning over me and smiling, "that ninety percent of your nerve endings are in your skin?"

"No," I say.

He turns to his nurse, who is holding down my arm. "It's true. That's why this novocaine injection isn't going to hurt you."

"Why's that?"

"Because I'm injecting it *under* the skin."

I feel a hot, sharp buzz of pain. "OW!"

"You see—nothing at all."

Ha, ha, I think. A comedian no less.

I am a fortunate young lady. Miraculously, I missed my tendon. Although I must see Dr. Greenspan in his office at noon on Tuesday, the day after tomorrow, I can leave now, with six stitches beneath a bandage so fat I look like I just returned from combat in Korea.

Out on the sidewalk the heat is unreal. We decide to buy a *Post*, find an air-conditioned restaurant, and go to a movie, in that order. The apartment will be depressing, not to mention hot.

Very slowly, we drive down Fifth Avenue.

15

THE NEXT DAY I WAKE
up more depressed than ever and covered with
sweat. My hand aches dully. In the kitchen is a note
from my father and two pills. The note says: "Pooh:
take these (aspirin and codeine) for pain. I'll be out
at 11:50." As I am swallowing the aspirin and codeine, the buzzer sounds in the kitchen. This just
means that a patient has rung the bell and walked
into the office, and during the winter I get used to
it. Now it makes me jump, and the pills get stuck
in my throat. Could things possibly be worse?

Our apartment looks unreal. The blinds are all
down, and slipcovers with garish flowers protect the
furniture. Since the maid cleans only once a week

in summer, an even film of dust covers the polished surfaces of everything.

When my father comes out of his office, he asks if I'm well enough to run an errand for him. The jeweler at 82nd Street and Broadway will have his watch repaired by three o'clock. The address is on the ticket, which he gives me in an envelope with ten dollars. Five is for the watch, the other five for me. I tell him I don't want five dollars. I don't deserve it. He insists, as a favor to him, and suggests I buy some books. I'll have plenty of time to read.

Going down in the elevator, all I can think is how much I wish John would come home. I would do anything to see him.

Outside it's like a furnace. People move in slow-motion, their heads tilted slightly forward, like flowers on wilted stems. My hand is throbbing, and I can't remember what it ever felt like to be cool or not in pain. On Broadway, an old lady trembles under a black umbrella. Above her the time, now 3:30, alternates with the temperature, a steady 96°.

In Womrath's I buy a collection of short stories by Ernest Hemingway and Jack London's *White Fang*. I resolve to study these books and learn the secret of indomitable will. Outside, the fruit vendor's bony horse, dozing at the curb, makes me want to cry.

Now and then someone can be heard wondering aloud if it's hot enough for someone else.

At the jeweler's, my father's watch, now ticking off the passing seconds faithfully, says exactly four o'clock. "You tell him no more swimming in this one," says the jeweler, raising his eyebrows to let a monocle fall from one eye.

"Is that what happened?"

"Tell him I have just the right watch for him. Inexpensive and guaranteed waterproof to forty feet."

"I'll tell him," I say. "Thanks."

Returning from Broadway to Central Park West means walking uphill, away from the river, toward the high ground in the center of Manhattan Island. I walk slowly, reflecting on my father's careless treatment of his watch. It's the kind of behavior *I* am famous for. I pass Amsterdam Avenue and the building where we lived for ten years, where it snowed Johnson's Baby Powder and I was happy.

Approaching the corner of Central Park West, I see Timothy crossing 86th Street. It is amazing: just as when I first saw him on the beach, I lose my sense of being connected to the ground. Fear has made my knees fluid, and adrenaline is shooting through my muscles. I feel I am about to rise into the air.

What's happening? What's he doing here? What if John came home while he was hanging around?

I dash around the corner and watch him walk right to the awning of our building, wave to the doorman, and go inside. I rush down the block and into the front hallway. I can't think why I should be so frantic. John won't be back for at *least* a week. I know this, and I'm still panicked. Why?

Timothy sees me skidding to a halt just as the elevator arrives. He turns suddenly pale. I stumble forward and bump into my father's 3:40 patient with my bandaged hand. I cry, "OW!"

"Oh, dear!" she cries. "I'm so sorry."

"No!" I tell her, "*I*'m sorry. It's all my fault, believe me!"

"Are you all right?" she wants to know.

I feel like shouting, "No! I'm dying, help!" but instead I say, "Oh, sure, absolutely!" and back into the elevator. Timothy follows me in. The doors close.

I stare at the numbers as they light up above the door. Timothy stares at the floor. Then I stare at the floor, and he stares at the numbers. My heart is pounding so hard I think the elevator man must hear it.

We arrive. The doors open, and all at once my dream of the other morning comes back to me, whole and in a flash: Timothy—the patient in the dentist's office!

I can no longer deny what I have obviously known all along.

The elevator departs. I feel a rush of seasickness and turn, trembling to Timothy, who is standing at the office door, about to ring the bell and walk in. "You should have told me who you *were*!" I scream in a whisper.

"Come off it," he says, and goes inside.

In a daze, I move to my sister's windowsill, wondering how a person can have feelings like this without dying. That's what I can't understand. Or passing out or something—screaming—but I couldn't.

All I would like is to find a cave somewhere, deep in the rocks where my father couldn't find me. I would hide out like a fox injured by a trap. Wild animals would be my friends. I'd wear a leopard skin and run with the pack, hunt and learn how to take care of myself. . . .

141

When my father comes out of his office, he goes straight to the bar and pours himself a drink.

Then he enters my sister's room and looks at me.

I cannot decipher his feelings from his face, which is nearly without expression, like Governor Harriman on the six o'clock news. I realize that my posture—slumped on the windowsill—has given me a horribly stiff neck.

He sits down on a chair in the middle of the room in light that is not exactly dim, but not exactly bright. He doesn't say anything.

A million thoughts are clamoring to get into my mind at once. In the din I can't hear any one of them clearly, and it's giving me a headache. I sigh.

He looks up.

I look down.

He clears his throat.

Inside, my mind is like a crazy circus with all the acts happening at once. It is chaos. Insanity.

If only I could be a little girl again, too small to be responsible, too innocent to be punished. I was so cute at three. I remember getting my first coloring book and a set of crayons. I went wild, gleefully scribbling all over the pages, in an ecstasy of creative delight. When I was finished, about five minutes after I began, I shouted for my mother to come and see. She said, "Oh, it's beautiful! Let's show it to your father." We showed it to my father. My father looked at it, and then he looked at me, and said, "Don't you know you have to stay inside the lines?"

The truth is I hadn't even *considered* having to stay inside the lines. Having to stay inside the lines changed everything. The scene is so vivid in my mind. I looked from the coloring book to him and from him to the coloring book, and my creations, which had just been so miraculous, turned into monstrosities. Then I did what any totally humiliated, disappointed, disillusioned three-year-old would do: I screamed. After I finished screaming, I ripped all the pages out of my coloring book and savagely destroyed them.

Now my father is going to remind me that in life, as in coloring books, you have to stay inside the lines. Even though it's what he's got to do, I hate him for it.

He sighs. "All right, what went on between the two of you? I think I have a right to know."

There is no question of telling the truth. "Nothing," I say.

"Okay, Winifred. I want some straight answers now and I'm not kidding."

I do not like his attitude. I try being civil. "I met him on the beach is all. I was taking a walk."

"You canNOT mean to tell me you didn't know who he was!" he says indignantly. "I mean, forchristssake, you rode up in the *elevator* with him, didn't he even look familiar?"

"NO! I mean . . ."

"What *do* you mean?"

"He said I'd seen him the night before, at the movies, only I couldn't remember, but I didn't really think about it."

"WHAT?" he cries, tossing the remnants of his composure to the wind. "You didn't *think* about it?"

I'm trapped, I see. It's time to turn and fight.

"NO! I didn't think about it because it didn't seem *important!*"

His jaw is working visibly. His lips are tight and white around the edges. "It didn't *what?*" he yells. "I find this *most disturbing.*"

"Well, that's your goddamn problem," I shout, "because nothing *happened!*"

Suddenly he smashes his glass onto the marble coffee table and it shatters into smithereens. "Father!" I say, stunned.

He seems not to notice the broken glass or that his hand is wet with alcohol and little drops of blood. "As *I* understand it," he says, "a very great *deal* happened. Which is precisely why it disturbs me to hear you say that *nothing* happened!"

"You're making me feel terrible!" I tell him.

"That's not my fault," he snaps, taking out his handkerchief and mopping at the mess on the table.

"It's your impulsiveness that drives me crazy," he says, looking for the first time at his hand, which is bleeding slightly in several places. "You overlook the crucial details. You could sleepwalk through a hurricane. Now, I want to know what happened, Winifred. And I want to know now."

If I tell the truth, he's liable to call Bellevue and ask the men in white coats to come pick me up, I know it. What if he knew about the drive in the Thunderbird? Or that night Timothy had his hand practically in my *crotch?* God! "We just talked a lot," I say breathlessly. "Actually, *he* talked a lot, like about his parents dying and his uncle."

"His parents dying," my father repeats.

"And I felt sorry for him, that's all."

144

"What did he say his name was?"

"Timothy Wilding III."

"You don't say. And you believed everything he told you, naturally. How did he say his parents died?"

I'm getting a little nauseous. "I don't remember," I say.

"So far," my father says, "none of what he said is true."

"Does he have a twin sister?" I ask, suddenly anxious, on the run.

"You amaze me! Not only did he tell you lies, he told you *cheap* lies, obvious trans*parent* lies."

The degree of self-contempt I am experiencing is unreal. It's as though I had been lured into a dark alley by the classic seedy pervert with an ice-cream cone. I feel not only foolish, but somehow tarnished.

My father says: "I think you should know he's been dropped from analysis."

This is so shocking I lose my balance completely. "Very funny," I say. "Ha, ha."

My father looks up with an unmistakably serious expression. He has been dabbing intermittently at the little cuts on his hand. Now he opens the handkerchief and winds it into a bandage.

I am in despair. My resentment toward Timothy has drowned in a torrent of guilt. "Why?" I say. "Did you have to?"

"He violated the basic trust of our relationship. I've referred him to somebody else. I couldn't possibly help him now."

I don't know what to think any more, so I stop thinking.

There are only shadows, the noises of the city.

"GOD!" my father suddenly explodes, "I can't stand it!" There is anguish in his voice now. "I see it all," he continues. "I understand just what's going on with you. First, you fail to pay attention. Then, because you were distracted, you have to act on impulse. Do you know what I mean? I mean, it's dangerous to act when you don't know what's really going on. And so you get into trouble, make a mess, get everyone angry at you, and then hate yourself. Am I right?"

"Exactly," I say, wondering how he knows that.

"You're just like me," he sighs, shaking his head sadly. "Do you know that? *That's* what I can't stand."

For a dizzy moment I feel like I'm on the edge of a cliff that is collapsing fast. And there is only one thing I can do and that is make the leap to the next cliff. Except the distance is so vast.

Why have I never seen the pain behind my father's eyes before? It's so intense, how could I have missed it?

The ground has given way. Suddenly nothing makes sense. I tell him so.

"I know the pattern of your self-destructive behavior." He sighs. "Because you've gotten it from me. You've always identified with me."

"And that's why I hate myself?"

"I'm terribly afraid so."

"Do you hate yourself?"

"Part of me does."

"But, *Father*, you're the psychoanalyst."

"Please," he begs, "don't remind me."

146

16

ful in September; the air is unexpectedly clear.

With summer still reflected in their faces, people parade the streets in their new fall fashions. This year, I am not pleased to report, the emphasis is on *waists*. Cinch belts are everywhere, as are slinky sheath skirts, their hems up an inch from last spring.

Insane as usual, Diana invested $12.95 in something called a waist-cincher that pushes her up above and squeezes her in below and which she can hardly breathe in. I tried it on the other day while she was out. It was flattering; a strapless, lacy affair just right for Elizabeth Taylor to seduce Clark Gable in, though how she would manage to sit down in it is a mystery to me. When I took it off, after nearly ten minutes, there were red grooves on my ribs and stomach.

People are crazy. My mother walks around in heels higher and skinnier than ever. Luckily, her skirts are so slinky she can take only small steps. Otherwise, I'm sure she'd break her neck. Just to be beautiful. It doesn't make sense.

Certain things stay the same: Fidel Castro keeps fighting in Cuba; President Eisenhower plays golf.

Because the Russians launched Sputnik last year, school, when it begins, is going to emphasize more math and science. This is definitely not my idea of good news.

At home things are more or less normal. My mother complains that my father works too hard, and my father explains that he has to if he's going to support our family in the manner we've grown accustomed to. I hardly see him. When he isn't with his patients, he's going out with my mother to: cocktail parties, dinner parties, fund-raising dinner-dances, Carnegie Hall, the Russian Tea Room, Broadway musicals. They are either busy or exhausted.

My sister and I criticize their behavior continually: "... and did you see what she was *wearing*?!"

"God!"

"Can you ever in your whole life imagine going around in a dress that positively reveals your *breasts*, forheavensake?"

"Diana, you're exaggerating."

"Well, the tops of them then."

"No. But I"—sigh—"can't imagine having breasts to reveal either."

John came home with a good, old-fashioned case of poison ivy all around his eyes and on his arms and another place too embarrassing to mention. Because, he told me, the toxins get into your bloodstream and surface wherever there is a dense collection of veins near the skin. He knows, because he looked it up (which was very industrious of him). He looks puffy and Oriental. He's decided to go to medical school after all.

Four years of college, plus four years of medical school, a one-year internship, and three years as a resident accounts for the next twelve years of John's life. When I'm with him, I find myself adding it up. Or remembering what my father said about Worcester, Massachusetts, being the first place in America that Sigmund Freud ever spoke, about forty years ago. Or wondering who I will fall in love with when John leaves for Worcester, Massachusetts, next week.

I am praying there will be *someone*.

Not that I'm afraid of being lonely. What I'm afraid of is being bored. If I hadn't been so bored, I wouldn't have gotten involved with Timothy. Timothy may have been neurotic, but he certainly wasn't boring.

My father hasn't mentioned Timothy again. He did tell me to think about "talking to someone," though, which means seeing a psychoanalyst.

The trouble is all the psychoanalysts I think about

seeing are friends of my father's, so I can't imagine being too frank with them.

I wouldn't want to embarrass anyone, and psychoanalysts are easy to embarrass. Take my father. My father gets embarrassed if he happens to walk into my room when I'm getting dressed. If I walk into *his* room when *he's* getting dressed, it's even worse; he could easily break his neck tearing into the bathroom or leaping into the nearest closet.

In a way, my father would be the ideal person for me to talk to, because he *does* know me so well, and he knows about important stuff from my life that I can't even remember and, what is more, our problem is quite similar, apparently. But it could never work out, even if it weren't against the rules, just because we'd both be so embarrassed. In psychoanalysis you're not supposed to be embarrassed to say *anything*, but we still would be.

I don't even know *why* we'd be so embarrassed, but I bet it's like being guilty: something you learn from your parents who learned it from their parents until by now everyone just thinks it's part of the Human Condition.

I refuse to think of the Human Condition as all grim—even though it *is* pretty crazy. But if it weren't crazy lots of things probably wouldn't be half as exciting, most people wouldn't be nearly as interesting, and my father would be out of a job.

Hopefully things won't be so agonizing now that I understand more about what is really going on. My only concern is that everything could change again all of a sudden, as it always seems to—especially when it comes to things like sex.

WINIFRED ROSEN was born in 1943 and grew up in New York City. She has had five children's books published, most recently, *Henrietta, the Wild Woman of Borneo,* and she has written for *Harper's Magazine.* She now lives in Berkeley, California where she is writing and painting mandalas.